T0063563

Galactic Phrase Book & Travel Guide

THE STAR WARS LIBRARY
PUBLISHED BY DEL REY BOOKS

STAR WARS: THE ESSENTIAL READER'S COMPANION
STAR WARS: THE ESSENTIAL GUIDE TO WARFARE
STAR WARS: THE ESSENTIAL ATLAS
STAR WARS: JEDI VS. SITH: THE ESSENTIAL GUIDE TO THE FORCE
STAR WARS: THE NEW ESSENTIAL CHRONOLOGY
STAR WARS: THE NEW ESSENTIAL GUIDE TO ALIEN SPECIES
STAR WARS: THE NEW ESSENTIAL GUIDE TO CHARACTERS
STAR WARS: THE NEW ESSENTIAL GUIDE TO DROIDS
STAR WARS: THE NEW ESSENTIAL GUIDE TO VEHICLES AND VESSELS
STAR WARS: THE NEW ESSENTIAL GUIDE TO WEAPONS AND TECHNOLOGY

THE STAR WARS CRAFT BOOK
THE COMPLETE STAR WARS ENCYCLOPEDIA
A GUIDE TO THE STAR WARS UNIVERSE
STAR WARS: DIPLOMATIC CORPS ENTRANCE EXAM
STAR WARS: GALACTIC PHRASE BOOK AND TRAVEL GUIDE
I'D JUST AS SOON KISS A WOOKIEE: THE QUOTABLE STAR WARS
THE SECRETS OF STAR WARS: SHADOWS OF THE EMPIRE

THE ART OF STAR WARS: A NEW HOPE
THE ART OF STAR WARS: THE EMPIRE STRIKES BACK
THE ART OF STAR WARS: RETURN OF THE JEDI
THE ART OF STAR WARS: EPISODE I THE PHANTOM MENACE
THE ART OF STAR WARS: EPISODE II ATTACK OF THE CLONES
THE ART OF STAR WARS: EPISODE III REVENGE OF THE SITH

SCRIPT FACSIMILE: STAR WARS: A NEW HOPE
SCRIPT FACSIMILE: STAR WARS: THE EMPIRE STRIKES BACK
SCRIPT FACSIMILE: STAR WARS: RETURN OF THE JEDI
SCRIPT FACSIMILE: STAR WARS: EPISODE I THE PHANTOM MENACE

STAR WARS: THE ANNOTATED SCREENPLAYS
ILLUSTRATED SCREENPLAY: STAR WARS: A NEW HOPE
ILLUSTRATED SCREENPLAY: STAR WARS: THE EMPIRE STRIKES BACK
ILLUSTRATED SCREENPLAY: STAR WARS: RETURN OF THE JEDI
ILLUSTRATED SCREENPLAY: STAR WARS: EPISODE I THE PHANTOM MENACE

THE MAKING OF STAR WARS: EPISODE I THE PHANTOM MENACE
MYTHMAKING: BEHIND THE SCENES OF STAR WARS: EPISODE II ATTACK OF THE CLONES
THE MAKING OF STAR WARS: EPISODE III REVENGE OF THE SITH
THE MAKING OF STAR WARS
THE MAKING OF STAR WARS: THE EMPIRE STRIKES BACK
THE MAKING OF STAR WARS: RETURN OF THE JEDI

STAR WARS®

Galactic Phrase Book & Travel Guide

A Language Guide to the Galaxy*

Compiled by the Baobab Merchant Council
With the Generous Sponsorship of the Widows of
Alderaan Educational Consortium

BY EBENN Q3 BAOBAB

DEL REY
NEW YORK

*Galactic Standard Version; designed for humans and human systems only. For Guides
written in other languages, visit our Origin Scroll on the HoloNet by punching in
UUU.CEC.COR. Full telepathic inputs are also accepted, but no collect-charge cerebral
communication, please. Gonk, Gonk, Gonk ko kyenga see.

A Del Rey® Book
Published by The Random House Publishing Group

Copyright © 2001 by Lucasfilm Ltd. & ™.
All Rights Reserved. Used Under Authorization.

All rights reserved.

Published in the United States by Del Rey Books, an imprint of The
Random House Publishing Group, a division of Random House, Inc.,
New York, and simultaneously in Canada by Random House of Canada
Limited, Toronto.

Del Rey is a registered trademark and the Del Rey colophon is a
trademark of Random House, Inc.

www.starwars.com
www.starwarskids.com
www.delreybooks.com

Library of Congress Catalog Card Number: 00-193530

ISBN 0-345-44074-9

Interior illustrations by Sergio Aragonés
Interior design by Michaelis/Carpelis Design Assoc. Inc.
Cover illustration by Warren Fu, ILM Art Department

First Edition: August 2001

146122990

TABLE OF CONTENTS

PART ONE: THE PHRASE BOOK

INTRODUCTION 4

ABOUT THE AUTHOR 9

1 GREETINGS AND SALUTATIONS 13
Pre-Corellian
Huttese

2 SPACE TRAVEL 17
Bocce
Renting a Spacecraft in Bocce
Business and Executive Travel

3 SURVIVAL IN HUTTESE .31
Mos Eisley
Favorite Huttese Food and Drink
Hutt Arithmetic
Bargaining for Your Life, and Other Combat
    Situations

4 HOW TO DEAL WITH EWOKS 49
First Contact
Asking for Directions
The Spirit World of the Ewoks, and Other Cautions

5 COMMUNICATING WITH WOOKIEES 63
Getting Started
Wookiee Translators
Small Talk with Wookiees

6 THE BASICS WHEN IT COMES TO DROIDS 71
  Origins of Droidspeak
  Communicating with a Droid
  Additional Handy Droid Sound-Phrases
  A Special Note on Droidspeak Encryption

7 JAWAS CAN BE YOUR FRIENDS 79
  History of the Jawa Language
  Meeting Jawas
  Jawa Numbers and Measurements
  Renting from the Jawas

8 SAND PEOPLE OR WORSE 91

9 UNDERWATER WITH THE GUNGANS 95
  Old Gungan
  Visiting the Gungans
  Common Everyday Expressions

10 EXPOSING YOURSELF TO THE NEIMOIDIANS . . .105

11 GETTING A HAIRCUT 115

PART TWO: BEHIND THE SOUNDS . . .121
  Speaking in Tongues
  Going Backwards
  Voices from Space
  Little Aliens, Big Voices
  Alien "Character Actors"
  R2-D2: The Biggest Challenge

Star Wars: *Screening One*
Post–Star Wars
Huttese Comes of Age
A Twenty-Year Gap
The New Era

APPENDIX: SELECTED ALIEN
  LANGUAGE SCENES FROM
  STAR WARS 165
A NEW HOPE
RETURN OF THE JEDI

Galactic Phrase Book & Travel Guide

PART ONE

THE
PHRASE
BOOK

by Ebenn Q3 Baobab

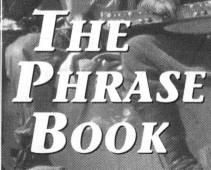

INTRODUCTION

It's been six standard years since the Battle of Yavin, and the tumult that engulfed much of the system has quieted down. Free travel is flourishing again. From the Galactic Core to the Outer Rim Territories, exploration, business, trade, and tourist ventures are whisking travelers across new frontiers and plunging them into diverse cultures. Perhaps you already have been, or are about to become, one of those daring voyagers.

Unless you own a protocol droid programmed to speak over six million languages, you are going to need some help to make yourself understood in your travels through the galaxy. A rudimentary understanding of certain languages is only the first step, though. You also need to learn as much as you can about alien cultures.

Get used to the idea that you are only a human, and there are a lot of strange beings out there that will behave quite differently from what you consider normal. You certainly don't want to embarrass yourself by inadvertantly offending another life-form—you might find yourself cast out into the back alleyways of Mos Eisley or, even worse, serving time aboard a Screed galley ship for insulting the wrong Hutt at the wrong moment! So you're going to need to make sure you know the basics of communication and good behavior.

I have traveled for forty-five seasons with the

Baobab Merchant Fleet and visited more than 1,300 distinct culture units. Despite the loss of the tip of my left foot and some permanent hair loss I experienced at a Hutt-Neimoidian peace conference, I have only gained from my travels.

Experience has shown that every human can master a basic set of alien phrases—although for some reason, in no part of the galaxy or in any language are adolescents able to master the phrase "May I help by washing the dishes?" Despite this strange vergence in the continuum, I believe there is hope out there that we can communicate with the enormous diversity of living protoplasm and cyber-sentient intelligence that surrounds us.

Each chapter in this guide includes essential cultural advice and rules of protocol that should be taken into account in various common situations. For example, always look a Jawa in the eyes, and ignore the strong odor. Simple phrases are presented that you will find essential in finding your way, obtaining or giving important information, and getting yourself out of trouble.

The emphasis will be on fundamental communication, and the average person fluent in Basic should have no problem being understood. Each simple phrase is printed out phonetically. For example, under "How to Deal With Ewoks" you will be given the Ewok phrase for

Can I have breakfast in my room?
Fingwa jo bifla o mi goontah?

as well as

No thank you, please, I can't swallow another
bark lizard.
***Netnoo ee goop-tah, Jee onko mee yuzi heeta
hutah.***

And of course, under "Space Travel" you will learn
the universal phrase all Hutt children know by heart:

Are we there yet?
Pee wom me doopee?

The answer—also in Huttese—is, naturally:

If you ask that one more time, I'm activating your seat
ejector!
Beeka doe wampa keejeckta peedunkey!

That's generally enough to quiet any protest.
The critical information found in the text will
provide you with a veritable compendium of unique
phrases, advice, and facts that normally would be
learned only by the most experienced traveler. For
example, do you know:

During space flight, you *never* ask "May I open
the window?" in any language.

The most common Huttese phrase used by any
visitor in Mos Eisley is:

When does the next bus leave?
Dipyuna co pana Gupankee?

The second most common phrase is:

I didn't order this!
Mee dwanna go stupa!

And the third most common phrase is:

I've lost a filling!
O wamma wonka!

This phrase book will cover the most likely situations that galactic travelers find themselves in, including basic language for:

- Greetings and salutations
- Travel and accommodations
- Asking directions
- Barter and purchases
- Shopping, ordering food, and eating
- Combat situations
- Bargaining for your life

Whether you are doing business with the Hutts or just getting your hair done, this book is for you. The languages covered in this guide include:

- Bocce
- Droidspeak
- Ewokese
- Gunganese
- Huttese
- Jawaese
- Neimoidian

- Shyriiwook (Wookiee-speak)
- Sullustan
- Tusken

Remember, learn the facts and the phrases well, and your chance of survival is increased by an enormous percentage. Just imagine the excitement that lies ahead for you. You will have the profound pleasure of being able to understand and communicate with pilots, bounty hunters, speeder drivers, waiters, lawyers, and old aliens sitting on park benches.

Ebenn Q3 Baobab
Chief Philologist
Baobab Archives, Manda

ABOUT THE AUTHOR

Ebenn Q3 Baobab, perhaps better known as EQ3, is the distinguished author, traveler, humorist, adventurer, historian, and philologist. Famed for possessing the largest private collection of Hutt folk art from the pre-Slime era, he is also known to millions throughout the Galactic Core by way of his popular broadcasts on the Baobab HoloNet, which spread his charm, political and cultural acumen, keen social insights, and holiday cookie recipes directly into the dwellings of viewers everywhere.

He is also the author of five books, the most famous being *The Secret of Joy in the Galaxy* and the bestselling *Repair Guide to Vaporators*. In addition, he has written an autobiography, two collections of short stories, and five volumes of poetry, twice earning the coveted Laureate of the Empire.

His rise to scholar began when he was only ten years of age. He left a promising career as an acrobat with his family's circus and embarked alone on the first of his epic wanderlusts across the galaxy. He began his new life as a cabin boy on a Baobab caravel. Writing daily in his life journal, EQ3 wrestled with innate melancholia by musing on the rainbow sunsets of Bantu, the skies of Roon darkened by great mynock migrations, and the innocent and joyful babble of baby Rodians in the Kibanyas on Tatooine.

He jumped ship somewhere near Biitu, but was captured and pressed into infantry service, first by the Moras, and later by the Hutts during the Koong

Wars. He became a fierce warrior, as well as a poet and mathematician. Eventually escaping, he returned to the merchant service as a ship's doctor with the Neimoidian Fleet. He was one of only two survivors aboard the minesweeper *Rodrigo Andrera* when it self-detonated during the cleanup of the Palpatine Mine Network. He fought the Kinkees with Captain Gordun during the Aerial Plankton Uprising and was instrumental in exposing the Endor Moon Hoax. He dined with the Lost Sultans of Lust and was the driving force behind the retrieval, restoration, and display of the Great Heep, which is today on permanent exhibit in the Baobab Museum of Science. All of these magnificent adventures are colorfully described with breathtaking lyricism and unflagging power in his autobiography, *Blazing Rockets*.

As a result of his epic voyages, EQ3 became deeply versed in the languages and cultures from the Outer Rim to the Galactic Core. From planet to planet he fought, loved, painted, composed music, and entertained at private parties as he experienced day-to-day survival in a multitude of alien cultures. In short, he became one of the most widely cultivated human beings in the system.

Today, he lives quietly in a villa on his home planet, Manda, with his wife, Pookie, and a miniature bantha named Nuke. EQ3 and Pookie have four grown children and eighteen adored grandchildren.

He is one of the few living authors that tempt us to use superlatives. He is the bright light of our era.

—The Publisher

GREETINGS AND SALUTATIONS

Making a good first impression is always important when meeting new life-forms. A casual wave of the hand, however, or extension of an arm for a handshake may result in the loss of your limb. So it is generally best to approach each new specimen slowly but confidently, keeping one hand ready to draw your weapon—if you are armed—and an eye open for a quick escape route should trouble come your way. Try to determine quickly just how many eyes and appendages you are dealing with, and make sure you recognize the front from the back. I've had many reports of travelers painfully mistreated by involuntary defense mechanisms on the backside of what was otherwise a friendly creature.

This chapter will give you the most probable phrases you need to greet a diversity of life-forms. The particular languages covered here are the most widespread in the galaxy, and chances are, someone will understand you. More specific and localized languages, such as Ewokese or Jawaese, for instance, are dealt with in detail in their own sections.

PRE-CORELLIAN

The most universal intergalactic greeting is derived from the ancient pre-Corellian salutation **yaa-yaah**. This sound is recognized by almost all air-breathing life-forms who vocalize by bellowing air from their lungs through a resonant vocal cavity. This phrase can be accompanied by a soft gesture of the right hand slightly extended with open hand palm downward. Even strictly visual communicators and most telepathic forms seem to understand this phrase when combined with the accompanying gesture. Note, though, that there is one known exception: Ugnaughts, common to Bespin and other Tibanna gas mining planets, take this as a personal insult and often respond by immediately hurling tools. Greet an Ugnaught by bowing silently, then await a guttural purring sound as a positive response. Otherwise, get ready to duck and roll.

Greetings.
Yaa-yaah.

To bid farewell, repeat the hand gesture and bow the head slightly. Use the ancient derivative of **yaa-yaah** for good-bye.

Farewell.
Haa-yaah.

Both the above phrases are recognized as peaceful and respectful forms of salutation throughout the galaxy.

HUTTESE
Whether we like it or not, so much business is done with the Hutts that a basic knowledge of that language is essential, especially for the executive and business traveler. More will be covered later in the chapter devoted to Huttese, but here are the basic salutations to get you started.

Greetings.
H'chu apenkee.

I am a friend.
Dolpee kikyuna!

I am pleased to meet you.
Mee dunkee gunko.

Take me to your leader.
Geebawa do lorda numa.

Or, if the situation is a bit tense:

I come in peace.
Nee dolya pukee toba.

In a more formal situation—for example, meeting a Hutt lord:

Greetings, glorious host.
H'chu apenkee, o' grandio lust.

CHOWBASO.

If you are the host:

Welcome.
Chowbaso.

A common farewell:

Good-bye.
Mee jewz ku.

Or, if more formality is needed:

May your juices stay fresh.
Twoos pa reeta bah flootah.

This is the best translation I can give of this antique Huttese idiom. Delivered with the proper air of humility, it expresses a profound respect for authority.

2 | SPACE TRAVEL

Thanks to the absence of open warfare in the space lanes, and the dry-docking of Imperial Interdictor cruisers responsible for pulling craft out of hyperspace during the recent Rebellion, you may be among the many who find it relatively safe and economical to cross space again.

Tourism has increased tenfold over the past three standard years, stimulated in a major way by the private acquisition of *Lambda*-class shuttles. This flood of new transport ships came about when an Imperial StarTrain container was abandoned after the Battle of Endor, with 300 new factory-sealed shuttles on board. Auctioned to the private trade sector and repainted in colorful holiday themes, these ships spurred immediate growth in the tourist industry. But the traveler should beware of unqualified drivers. Just last year, two shuttles carelessly spun into the Fusion Clouds of Tartaglia and were stranded without fuel while chasing the annual migration of mynocks to the wind turbines on the asteroid Akatoa. This accident was attributed to the overzealous demands of picture-taking tourists on a novice pilot. So please be cautious.

BOCCE

Obviously, unless you are able to fold time organically, you will be traveling to your destination by spacecraft. Let's assume you are a passenger on one of the shuttles, starliners, or intercommerce vessels that follow the standard trajectories. Aside from Basic, you will need a knowledge of Bocce, the inter-system trade jargon developed by the Baobab merchants. Bocce was developed so there would be a common language among the highly diverse species of pilots and their crews. With just a few Bocce phrases you can communicate to any member of the crew or service personnel tendering your flight.

Hello.
Jettoz.

Where is my seat?
Infinez tope ur nockneez?

That ——— is in my seat.
(for example: Gamorrean pig guard)
Cee Gammor peeg feeth ur nockneez.

Can you turn the gravity down a little?
Peez doz gravorti dow pinti?

Can you turn the gravity up a little?
Peez doz gravorti oop pinti?

Thank you.
Zanki.

Will we be jumping to hyperspace?
Tuz de ju mugee hyperspaaze?

When are we going to get there?
Hwen dorix bijunize?

I am spacesick.
Meez peeza peeza.

My neighbor is spacesick.
Zee dopi peeza peeza.

Yes.
Keezx.

No.
Nokeezx.

Where is my luggage?
Infinez topi lopiz?

When will my luggage be here?
Hwen zu lopiz bobize?

That was my luggage.
Jaaz maz lopiz eyapopiz.

I have insurance.
Kazz ma kazz.

Good day (good-bye).
Koo-loozi.

For those of you piloting your own craft, a knowledge of Bocce will be necessary if you are to deal with navigational and technical issues. My suggestion would be to purchase a vocabulator for direct translation from Basic to Bocce on your onboard computer. This would assure the best safety margin.

However, if you are faced with voice communication, here are some handy priority phrases.

This is ——— (name your spacecraft).
Demeezz bo treeza ———.

Do you speak Basic?
Bazi batza Bazic?

Affirmative.
Yezzo.

Negative.
Noza.

Roger.
Rozah.

How far to ——— (name your destination)?
Butimoz hiz ———?

What are your coordinates?
Motex coff hupiz?

What are my coordinates?
Motex coff keez hupiz?

Can you send a pilot to guide me in?
Mii weez joto ne dimiix?

Emergency!
Vitteez!

Send help!
Geewaaz hokokeez!

Request landing coordinates, please.
Motex goy kiladez.

Request permission to enter landing zone.
Motex loriz cemik larhitazz.

I am approaching the landing zone now.
Kiz fiz dolomitex nuriz.

Clear the landing zone!
Kiz kiz fee dolomitex!

Move aside and stop hogging the space lane!
Jeeza goz dobo upinahex colax!

RENTING A SPACECRAFT IN BOCCE

Increasing numbers of rental agencies are appearing along the most common space lanes, so many since the Rebellion that you've probably heard that over-used phrase in Huttese, used by a traveler boasting of some physical abuse of a rented landspeeder or midsize drop ship:

It's only a rental!
Dopeelya puka!

This delinquency seems to be common to humans and aliens, especially Bothans. Nonetheless, the rental business is booming, despite the numerous insurance claims.

There's something very pleasurable about the interior, "new" smell of a rental—although when I leased one after two mudmen from Roon had used it for a weekend fling, the air was extremely foul. So before you make the deal, do a full olfactory scan.

Many rental agencies offer deep-space towing if you are so unfortunate as to get stranded. Most rentals will be fueled for only a fixed number of hyperspace jumps and are programmed to automatically return to base on the last jump. You pay up front for the number of jumps, and you should plan your itinerary accordingly. You likely will pay a big fine if you try to override the programming, and will find yourself in weekend flying school facing a dull and demanding Twi'lek instructor if you are convicted of jump-tampering the nav computer.

For sublight or planetary surface travel, rates are really good right now, due to the enormous Neimoidian discounts that have forced prices to drop everywhere. It's a good time to take that vacation to the floating cities of Calamari or to join the thousands of visitors making a Returning to the Graveyard of Alderaan.

Let's say you want to rent a Legion Condor EX. Here is what you would say:

I'd like to rent a Legion Condor EX.
Kizzee mit rentaz hu Legion Condor EX.

I want to purchase ——— jumps.
(two, four, six, eight, ten)
Meetic putzax ——— jumpes.
(zwoo, goor, zix, kata, atanox)

I want the collision insurance and medical coverage.
Meetix goyatoixee he manux ii mediizal.

I do not want the collision insurance and medical coverage.
Noy' meetix goyatoixee he manux ii mediizal.

I want a starchart of this sector.
Meetix hit y' starcharz o quadrux.

How do I exit this spaceport?
Deeza va deeza copex?

That scratch was there when I rented the ship.
Zat x'ratch keezo bompaz ha sheep.

BUSINESS AND EXECUTIVE TRAVEL

This section deals with what amounts to a rapidly
emerging class of business travelers who are having
a huge impact on services available across the
galaxy. We at the Baobab Archives Cultural Phenomenon Study Center haven't quite figured out why or
how this class of traveler sustains its existence, but
research is ongoing and we will be publishing a
thesis on the HoloNet in the near future. Needless
to say, we feel there is a definite need to service this
group of travelers, and so we have gathered together
a compendium of the most oft-used phrases, offered
here in both Bocce and Huttese. For each phrase
the first line is in Basic, then the same phrase is
offered in Bocce, and the third line is in Huttese.

I am a systems consultant.
Iyo waza goniteezex.
Dobra do poolyee yama.

I am a vice president and systems consultant for personnel development and management consulting.
Iyo waza kinateze u kuntatezaz u pizolooiz un tazax goniteezex.
Dobra do nupee nupee um baw wah du poolyee yama.

What do you do?
Finitez cetez detox?
Waki mallya kuna chu chu?

Here is the prospectus on systems and management consulting.
Hitermitex o spectus o goniteezex eh tazax goniteezex.
Noolee moolee bana kee cheel'ya cu kuna ku chu chu.

I will get back to you on that one.
Vitex fo gobaj ka zu zux.
La pim nallya so bata de wompa.

My droids will talk to your droids.
Keliza l'gik droi to talk droi.
Mwa droida bunno bunna droida.

The payment is in the HoloNet.
Ker pazet on bonip Holonot.
Beeska mu-moolee bu Halapu.

My program is faster because I have the latest moomaws.
Biztiz hit yilly rev moomaws.
Mwa pogwa dee kagwa mo moomaw.

Are there good drinks on board?
Openex co pakaz di hunhiy?
Cheska lopey x'hoo pumba?

Another hot towel, please.
Kitex co kopad nikozax, bleeze.
Andoba ne lappee, kolka.

An Aduki double, please.
Metox un Aduki dola, bleeze.
Banya kee fofo Aduki, momo.

Can I upgrade to first class?
Keez meeza foy wunclaz?
Cheesba hataw yuna puna?

May I have a receipt?
Tirez meez canto ripit?
Geebwa waa chimpa?

I'd like to check in.
Meeza copwat kiz eentock.
Kuna kee wabdah noleeya.

I'd like to check out.
Meeza copwat kiz oontock.
Kuna kee wabdah nenoleeya.

Will the bill list the title of the holo?
Beetix fo fee fi nototex ge holo?
Jeskawa no rupee dee holo woopee?

OPENEX CO PAKAZ DI HUNHIY?

COUNTING IN BOCCE

1	*wun*
2	*zwoo*
3	*treb*
4	*goor*
5	*fyiz*
6	*zix*
7	*zeve*
8	*kata*
9	*navax*
10	*atanox*
20	*gatanox*
50	*kimonex*
100	*pajono*
1,000	*apajono*
10,000	*opajono*

GLOSSARY OF COMMON BOCCE WORDS

accelerate	*acceleroz*
airlock	*airlox*
antigravity	*antegravorti*
arrival	*corox*
blast off	*blapdoz*
breath mask	*fazkup*
business class	*buzna klaz*
button	*pushee*
cargo	*omegi*
cockpit	*contulpit*
comet	*jestarx*
crater	*kradow*

cruiser	*kruza*
dampers	*dompaz*
departure	*decorox*
dock	*dok*
docking bay	*landar*
drink	*pakaz*
droid	*droi*
economy	*ekonix*
emergency	*egee*
exit	*va deeza*
explode	*ekraka*
fast	*rifflee*
fighter	*tacker*
fire	*fooma*
first class	*wunclaz*
force field	*forz fleed*
fuel	*octon*
gas	*jazt*
go	*ho*
gravity	*gravorti*
hatch	*hortch*
how	*huwax*
hyperdrive	*hypeergaz*
hyperspace	*hyperspaaze*
I	*meez*
ignition	*shastartaz*
land	*lande*
lift off	*shepe oop*
malfunction	*kadinger*
meal	*moma*
meteor	*varockee*

moon	*moana*
napkin	*lipwup*
now	*comda*
off	*uuf*
on	*ona*
orbit	*orbatex*
pillow	*peewa*
pilot	*capitona*
planet	*olando*
planetoid	*minolando*
police	*lawmapso*
power	*poe wa*
power converter	*poe wa vertaz*
release	*chee kutta*
retros	*retroz*
rocket	*rooka*
scope	*seepana*
seat	*nockneeze*
sensors	*zensaz*
shields	*zheelda*
shoot	*zootoo*
shut down	*uffdon*
signal	*zignale*
sleep	*hallaz*
slow	*nigwot*
space	*spaaze*
spacecraft	*spaaze zoomer*
space station	*spaaze forme*
spacesuit	*spaaze gomix*
star	*stuur*
start	*ignola*

stop	*storpa*
switch	*dunlix*
them	*yolats*
throttle	*handrex*
ticket	*otickee*
time	*timax*
towel	*kopad*
vacuum	*emtix*
viewscreen	*jeepeegee*
waste closet	*wapity pye*
we	*zeez*
weapon	*reapon*
what	*yapa*
when	*hwen*
where	*yureh*
who	*yoya*
why	*ewhy*
window	*lookaz*
you	*wox*

3 | SURVIVAL IN HUTTESE

As stated in chapter one of this guide, Huttese is so widespread that to travel and do effective business, you must possess some working knowledge of the language. Modern Huttese goes back more than 500 standard years. Its ancient origins, of course, can be traced to the Hutts on their native planet, Varl; the Baobab Archives have uncovered tablets in archaeological diggings on the moons of Varl showing ransom notes written in ancient Huttese at least 1000 years ago.

The modern language is hard to speak properly without ejecting and receiving some spittle, so just accept this as a natural necessity and persevere. Huttese is, unfortunately, a language spoken by the rougher, less-refined, and—let's face it—outright criminal element in the system.

You may often encounter a diverse group of Huttese-speaking life-forms all at once, in a market-place, a cantina, or a detention area. You may be abducted by some tribe or gang. If it's a hostile situation, common Huttese will almost certainly be understood by something in the crowd. Here are a few phrases to remember:

I am a friend!
Dolpee kikyuna!

Don't shoot!
Ap-xmasi keepuna! *(An X in Huttese is pronounced by making a wet snap of the lips, like an aggressive kissing sound.)*

Or, in a situation where you have the drop on a group of hostiles:

Everybody, hands off your weapons and back up against the bar!
Mikiyuna! Pasta mo rulya! Do bata gee mwaa tusawa!

Do you feel lucky, punk?
Dopo mee gusha, peedunkey?

Don't anybody move or the Wookiee here will tie your legs into a taut-line hitch!
Kickeeyuna mo Wooky doo tee puna puna! *(This phrase has been the saving grace for many a weary space tourist.)*

MOS EISLEY
It seems that sooner or later most space travelers having any business in the Outer Rim Territories end up passing through or making an extended stay in Mos Eisley or one of the other spaceports on Tatooine. Mos Eisley, once described as "a wretched hive of scum and villainy," has less scum nowadays. The recent cleanup has helped stimulate the tourist and business trade. Reports are that most of the virus-infected scurrier scum and graffiti have been

removed, and the vermin themselves have been caged up by Gardulla the Hutt and her minions. She apparently has plans to profit from their leathery pelts by creating a new product line in her notorious lingerie monopoly.

Since there is such a huge influx of foreign visitors to Mos Eisley, successful communication will also require accurate knowledge of the spaceport and places to lodge, eat, and shop if the traveler is to have a safe and successful stay. The following information comes from my translation of a recently published Huttese tour pamphlet, which highlights the features of what they refer to as "the quaint and colorful holiday oasis by the Dune Sea."

First, here are the best hotels in town:

The Dowager Queen
Jah Dowahga Kwee-Kunee
This well-known wreck of a spacecruiser has been remodeled into a first-class hotel, located right in the center of the spaceport. Make reservations in advance if possible, due to the popularity of this establishment for conventions and trade shows.

Motel Nebulus
Motal Nebuli
This past season they've had a great show in the nightclub here. The feature act presents Figrin D'an II and the New Modal Nodes, who have adapted their entire musical act to work underwater, in a big glass tank in the middle of the dance floor.

Hutt Chuba's
Hutt Chuba'z
Great place to order a cool Bantha Blaster at the end of a hot day and soak your toes in the Foamwander Spa. A hot spot to meet Mon Calamari.

Gardulla Oola
Gardulla Oola
Lots of cheap rooms, a casino, and a show featuring Dame Needa, the famous Oola impersonator, and the Adukis doing the famed Whirling Kavadango Dance.

For shopping, here are the biggest and the best markets and variety shops in Mos Eisley:

Tatooni Booka
Sells a huge variety of new and used data storage units, viewplates on all subjects, and recorded music in every format. It has a popular indoor reading court and café. This is the place where creatures meet creatures.

U Wanna Wanna
This is Mos Eisley's biggest outdoor market. Vendors offer unique foods and crafts. It is open year-round except during gravelstorms of magnitude four and above. It can be blisteringly hot. Remember to carry your angle-adjustable dual-dome umbrella to shade you from those twin suns.

Mo' Moolee Rah
This is a smaller open market affair, but offers unique used weapons and technical boutiques. This

is a good place for weapons maintenance and customizing. Located near the tough neighborhood of Tar Mass, this is not a place to go wandering about without adequate protection.

Bargoon Tatooni
The end may be in sight for this privately owned trading post. Rumors are, it will be engulfed into Barguna Moocha, the fabulously successful interstellar chain that is gobbling up private enterprise everywhere. Originally the site for the annual Jawa Rendezvous and Swap Meet, Bargoon Tatooni offers the best prices on used spaceship parts and cookware.

Here are the best Mos Eisley eating establishments:

Jeh Bonegnawer
Named after the infamous desert predator, the Bonegnawer offers an astounding array of live and prepared foodstuffs. Availability varies, but this is the place for specialties and imported foods. They maintain a sizable Corellian cuisine, and this is a good place to get your stomach back in equilibrium after too much exotic alien fare.

Buzzee's
Unique, entirely insect-based cuisine. Reasonable prices. Best larvae in the Outer Rim Territories.

Doe See'ybark Bootana
The Sail Barge Gardens
Some sections of Jabba the Hutt's demolished sail barge—heavily pockmarked with Nubian grapeshot—were used to form the interior walls of this restaurant.

With sunlight echoing down from skylights above, the place exudes a dappled grandeur. Good drinks and quiet booths make this a place of calm business and even romantic interaction. Very expensive, but will take pre- and post-Rebellion credits.

FAVORITE HUTTESE FOOD AND DRINK

In the event you end up as a guest in one of the Huttese establishments, you certainly want to avail yourself of the fine cuisine offered by the Hutt chefs. Despite many cultural inadequacies, the Hutts really know how to eat and drink.

To drink:
- Boga Noga
- Gardulla
- Tatooni Junko
- Yatooni Boska

All the above are mind-relaxing, to say the least. Two decanters of Boga Noga are enough to desensitize a squad of stormtroopers for the evening. Boga Noga also makes a great engine flush if poured directly into the fuel overflow valve of your speeder. I was thankful many a chilly desert morning for a few droobs of Boga Noga in my power converters. The magnetos turned over with a flash every time.

To eat:

strained keebadas
keebadas binggona

mubasa hock
mubasa hok

braised fork tarts
jimunee ronto pagona

scurrier tips (very seasonal)
scuzzi spits

SCUZZI SPITS

hot chubas
hotsa chuba

sand gizzars
sando g'dizzards

Hutt cuisine is somewhat casual, with bowls of
the above brought in and devoured in random order
amid a spray of drool. Utensils are optional. I would
recommend gloves, however. Sand gizzars are quite
abrasive, and the thorns on a fork tart can be painful.

In any event, these edible treasures are expensive.
This brings up the issue of Huttese accounting.

HUTT ARITHMETIC
Since the Hutts have eight fingers rather than the
human norm of ten, their system of counting is
base 8. This has led to much confusion when dealing with absolute numbers and historically has
given the Hutts a tricky advantage when negotiating
prices. For example, if a Hutt offers you twelve of
something, counting by Hutt standards, it will
amount to only ten of something in Basic. The skew

in perceived value increases rapidly as you count, as the following table illustrates.

COUNTING IN HUTTESE

Hutt Value	Huttese	Basic Value
0	*nobo*	0
1	*bo*	1
2	*dopa*	2
3	*duba*	3
4	*fwanna*	4
5	*k'wanna*	5
6	*keeta*	6
7	*goba*	7
10	*hunto*	8
11	*beeska*	9
12	*boboba*	10
13	*goboba*	11
14	*joboba*	12
15	*soboba*	13
16	*koboba*	14
17	*foboba*	15
20	*donocha*	16
21	*honocha*	17
22	*bohonocha*	18
23	*dohonocha*	19
24	*duhonocha*	20
144	*jujumon*	100

etc.

Numbers seem to increase more rapidly when one counts as a Hutt. A Hutt may offer you a given price for a deal, which is misleading, and you may be disappointed when the payoff comes.

A major cultural effect of Hutt base 8 has been the economic suppression of the Rodians by the Hutts. Rodians have ten fingers and evolved counting with base 10. When major Rodian land purchase contracts and communication franchises were set up, the Hutts took advantage of the confusion to basically squeeze out all Rodians from ownership. The result was their major financial subservience to the Hutts and the emergence of a nameless generation of Rodian lackeys.

Of course, there are other significant reasons why dealing with the Hutts can be nonprofitable, but a full explanation of those phenomena would take another whole book. Be cautioned! The Hutts are tricky. And slimy.

BARGAINING FOR YOUR LIFE, AND OTHER COMBAT SITUATIONS

With the sheer number of racketeers, bounty hunters, smugglers, and alien bad boys out there that converse in Huttese, the chances are quite high that at some point you are going to find yourself facing a threatening situation in which a knowledge of Huttese—and a fully charged E-11 on autofire—may be the only way out. Although we don't endorse provocation and violence, alas, it has proven essential to survival to harden one's language at the proper moment. For example:

Hey you!
Chuba!

Who are you?
Ah'chu apenkee?

What do you want?
Hi chuba da naga?

You're a low-down Imperial fool.
Kava doompa D'emperiolo stoopa.

Don't go for that weapon!
Hagwa boska punyoo!

Turn around real slowly.
Moova dee boonkee ree slagwa.

Keep your suction cups where I can see them.
Jeeska do sookee koopa moe nanya.

Shoot!
Keepuna!

You bother me.
Kee baatu baatu.

Going somewhere?
Koona t'chuta?

Drop your weapon.
Kee hasa do punyoo.

Don't move!
Hagwa doopee.

Smile when you say that.
Smeeleeya whao toupee upee.

Hands up.
Kapa tonka.

Tentacles up!
Tonta tonka.

You're in trouble now.
Bona nal kuchu.

It's too late.
Soong peetch alay.

You gonna pay for that?
U wamma wonka?

What took you so long?
Coona tee-tocky malia?

You disappoint me.
Keel-ee calleya ku kah.

Kill me, and ten more will rise in my place.
Je killya um pasa doe beeska wumpa.

The last fool who called me that got his antennae
stuffed down his throat.
***Da beesga coo palyeeya pityee bo tenya go kaka
juju hoopa.***

Why haven't you paid me?
Wanta dah moolee-rah?

When can I expect payment?
Wa wanna coe moulee rah?

I've got the credits.
Ting cooing koo soo ah.

What are you doing here?
Kee chai chai cun kuta?

There will be no deal.
Bargon wan chee kospah.

Give it to me.
Cha wana do bota.

You are my kind of scum.
U kulle rah doe kankee kung.

Don't count on it, slimeball.
Cha skrunee do pat, sleemo.

You weak-minded fool.
Coo ya maya stupa.

You will be rewarded.
Bargon u noa a-uyat.

Let's go.
Boska.

Out of my way.
Pushee wumpa.

Take him away.
Yacha neechu.

Bring her to me.
Koose cheekta nei.

Forward march.
Nudd chaa.

My lord.
Ma lorda.

Hopefully you won't need to use too many of the above phrases, and can get by with a more polite and civilized vocabulary, such as:

Greetings.
H'chu apenkee.

Welcome.
Chowbaso.

Good-bye.
Mee jewz ku.

Incredible!
Inkabunga!

Okay.
Eniki.

Yes.
Tagwa.

No.
Nobata.

Thank you.
No equivalent in Huttese.

Please
No equivalent in Huttese.

And here are some other appropriate phrases you may need to know:

How much is a room for the night?
Kava nopees do bampa woola?

I want the Hutt-size bed.
Jee oto ta Huttuk koga.

I will pay with credit. Here is my card.
Jee ho poka foo creeda. Vota myo creeta.

I would like room service.
Jee vopa du mooljee guma.

Can I visit the band backstage?
Kavaa kyotopa bu banda backa?

Can I visit the dancers backstage?
Kavaa kyotopa bu whirlee backa?

I will keep my weapon.
Jee oto vo blastoh.

Hello, my name is ———.
Achuta, my pee kasa ———.

How much for that item?
Kava che copah?

I'm not going to pay that!
Ees hoppoda nopa!

What's your final offer?
Hi chunkee fa goota?

Is that authentic?
Laboda na rowka?

Does that come with a warranty?
Va foppa gee wontahumpa?

Is this freshly dead?
Ne ompee doe gaga punta?

Do you offer vegetarian cuisine?
Chesko yo ho kimbabaloomba?

Is there a smoking section?
Tee ava un puffee lumpa?

Does this cause brain damage?
Dopa na rocka rocka?

GLOSSARY OF COMMON HUTTESE WORDS

activate	*rundee*
bargain	*bargon*
bet	*buttmalia*
boss	*lorda*
bounty hunter	*murishani*
boy	*peedunkee*
burp	*howdunga*
buy	*bedwana*
cake	*waffmula*
cheat	*cheeska*
contract	*nibobo*
dancing girl	*chik youngee*

dessert	*lickmoomoo*
die	*nee choo*
drink	*yocola*
droid	*droi*
drool	*sleemo poy*
enjoy	*panwa*
fool	*stupa*
friend	*pateessa*
go	*bolla*
gun	*wanga*
here	*wata*
home	*bunky dunko*
how	*kava*
I	*Jee*
idiot	*koochoo*
Imperial cruiser	*D'emperiolo teesaw*
Jedi	*Jeedai*
joke	*na yoka*
kidnap	*jujiminmee*
kill	*killee*
meal	*yafullkee*
message	*wankee*
money	*moulee-rah*
move	*yatuka*
naptime	*hunka be*
outlander	*ootmian*
pay	*wamma*
payoff	*makacheesa*
pie	*patogga*
planet	*planeeto*
Podrace	*choppa chawa*

power	*pawa*
price	*che copah*
ransom	*gopptula*
sell	*dwana*
slave	*shag*
sleep	*winkee*
smuggler	*ulwan*
snack	*smak telia*
space	*doma toma*
spaceship	*pankpa*
steal	*moocha*
them	*hoohah*
time	*tee-tocky*
we	*Jee-jee*
what	*haku*
when	*joppay*
where	*konchee*
who	*coo*
wine	*gocola*
you	*uba*

Mastery of Huttese can come only with extensive exposure to fluent speakers of the language. Some of the best teachers of the language have been those long-term hostages who have really had a unique opportunity to immerse themselves in the language for a period of two standard years or more. Several of these survivors have tenured as professors at the Baobab School of Speed-Learning, and their Huttese classes are continually wait-listed with eager students.

4 HOW TO DEAL WITH EWOKS

The Ewoks, one of the most remote and isolation-ist tribal units in the galaxy, are confined solely to the Forest Moon of Endor. A voyage to Endor requires a complicated series of hyperspace jumps from the Galactic Core, and once you arrive you should be prepared for living in the open for a long time before you ever see one of these shy creatures. You will want to plan on catching or carrying all your own food, or taking trade items in the hope that you will make Ewok contact and can barter for meals before you starve.

Nonetheless, since the Battle of Endor, there has been much historic sightseeing and souvenir hunt-ing on Endor, since the remains of the second Death Star and a multitude of crashed Imperial and Alliance warships lie decaying in the vast forests. There have been several privately funded salvage expeditions to retrieve valuable hardware, the most significant being the hire and transport of 480 Jawas from Tatooine to lend their salvaging skills to clean up wreckage. Last reports indicate they mutinied and formed a roving bandit gang that has been known to prey upon innocent visitors. No one has been hurt, but the theft of small unattended property, and the ugly swarms of nonnative Sinus Flies brought inadvertently with the Jawas—and reproducing unchecked due to the absence of natural predators—can dampen the fun of your visit. So it is advisable that preparation for a visit to Endor should include learning some basic Jawaese and bringing a healthy supply of Sinus Fly repellent.

FIRST CONTACT

Experience has shown that Ewoks are always approachable, and a smile, however stiff, is returned in kind. They tend to poke spears in your direction, but don't panic—it's their way of showing interest. Continued poking accompanied by chanting **"Ooloo, ooloo,"** however, means they are sizing you up for a meal. In case this happens, you need to exhibit your power and dominance over them by exploiting their superstitious nature. It's a good idea to carry a supply of cheap magnetic trinkets and reflective objects to impress them, and a few key phrases will help a great deal:

Greetings! I am a friend.
Yaa-yaah! Nude-La jeerota.

Or, in a less formal fashion:

Hi.
Goopa.

Thank you, I would love to visit your village.
Teeha, Meechoo nub hii vootok.

Beware, I have great power!
Che womok! Bont nub paamuk!

Blessings on your fowl.
Kiney chattu toma tip-yip.

I must go now.
Meechoo che donno moktok.

Thank you for your kind hospitality.
Teeha dupav vay kommah.

Good-bye.
Yeha.

These handy phrases should get you out of the boiling pot and on friendly terms. The next step in your relationship may involve bartering, and so:

Can we make a trade?	No.
Ya ees ma goo?	**Den.**
I want that one.	Hello.
Nenga ninga.	**Sku.**
How much?	That's too much.
Labu labu?	**Dee fratta oh chuck.**
I will give you this one.	That's not enough.
Oody eshtee a hat chaaa.	**Dee fratta choo doo.**
Yes.	Okay, you have a deal.
Chak.	**Acha, amoowa nocka.**

In general, Ewoks are a warm, loving life-form and will make loyal friendships. Their children are raised with great respect and pride for the forest habitat and have a profound understanding of the flora and fauna of their arboreal world. Once a good relationship has been established, you can put the Ewoks at even greater ease by incorporating some of the more common colloquialisms into your speech.

Hooray.
Yubnub.

Wow! *or* Gee whiz!
Ee chee wa maa!

Okay.
Acha.

Hey!
Ee choya!

Go.
Treek.

Let's go.
Yub yub.

Stop.
Na goo.

Fooey.
Kvark.

It is a sign of peace and contentment to chant what is more or less an ancestral folk song praising the forest for its great offerings. Give it a rambling musical contour.

Dugun duca lula ludla nuna, dounga, luna nudla.
alt. **Du-can du-can duca.**

Ultimate acceptance by the tribe will be indicated by the offer of food treats and meals. Ewoks work hard to gather and grow their foodstuffs, and it is truly a hospitable gesture for them to share their hard-earned supplies. Be prepared, however, for some unusual offerings. Politely refuse any bark lizard—it seems to cause involuntary tooth rash in most humans. And remember these phrases:

Yes, I am hungry.
Chak. Meechoo iyo bugdoo.

What dish is this?
Abbija goo boo?

I like it.
Yun yum.

It is very good.
Yun yum di goot.

May I have more, please?
Gyeesh. Manna maana mo wuhah?

I am satisfied now. Thank you.
Meechoo tee noot. Teeha.

Please, no more bark lizard.
Gyeesh, chak heeta hutah.

May I have something to drink?
Chiotto bat flingo lah?

May I have water, please?
Chiotto gyeesh ah-ah?

COUNTING IN EWOKESE

1	**chu**	6	**n'dla**
2	**fic**	7	**voo**
3	**chim**	8	**j'voo**
4	**hoji**	9	**coki**
5	**n'la**	10	**eedeeza**

ASKING FOR DIRECTIONS

Should you be passing through Ewok territory and need guidance, remember:

I am lost.
Chi ita lungee.

Where is the clearing?
Ne gata ke pi oto pibooka?

Where is the landing platform?
Ne gata fop ronda ronda?

Which direction does the sun rise from?
Noroway bi toto ka sunee re fopa?

Which direction is the upper polar cap?
Noroway bi toto ka pola cupee de oppra?

Can you guide me to the Death Star ruins?
Coro bingee me ota ji rueenee Death Star?

Can you guide me to the power station ruins?
Coro bingee me ota powa stoja rueenee?

THE SPIRIT WORLD OF THE EWOKS, AND OTHER CAUTIONS

The Ewoks believe that all life sprang from the Spirit Tree, and that all life spirits eventually return to this tree. This is a sacred site for them and is rarely shown to visitors. Whatever you may believe, it is important to honor their beliefs and treat any spiritual activity by the tribe with proper respect.

It is commonly speculated that as a result of the recent battle, a cloud of residual dark-side energy hovers in the vicinity of the Endor moon, so there is a modest risk of bad behavior by any life-forms who pass through the region. We had a report that last season a rowdy band of university students on holiday had enjoyed too much blumfruit cooler and accidentally extinguished the Ewok lantern of sacred light with a water balloon. This created an awkward incident, to say the least, so don't expect much access to the Spirit Tree until the memory of this event has faded.

Can you take me to the Spirit Tree?
Coro way nim-nee ash Kna Naa?

I respect the wishes of the Council of Elders.
Ninga ninga kee Treeta Dobra.

Celebrate the love.
Allayloo ta nuv.

Celebrate the freedom.
Coatee-cha tu yub nub.

Celebrate the power.
Coatee-cha tu paamuk.

Other common Ewok expressions include:

Alas!	Okay/All right.
Yut ehda!	***Acha.***
Giddyap.	Please.
Kaiya.	***Gyeesh.***
Good-bye.	Right/correct.
Yeha.	***Yesh.***
Hang on.	What happened?
Grenchicit.	***Tyeht danti?***
Hurray!	What's going on?
Yubnub!	***Kush drojh?***
Oh dear/Oh my.	Yipes!
Deksh.	***Eeep!***

GLOSSARY OF COMMON EWOK WORDS

arrow	***dutak***
axe	***eekeetuhkuh***
baby/child	***theesa***
beautiful	***luu***
be careful	***danvay***
berry	***sleesh***

big	*ekla*
branch	*jarat*
bring/fetch	*chesl*
brother	*fruk*
cave	*kreeth*
circle	*fulu*
climb	*yuf*
come	*tyatee*
cook	*entzahee roda*
cup	*yiyult*
dance	*reh rehluu*
danger	*hutar*
door	*sirut*
down	*jad*
drink	*gleeg*
dumb/silly	*lurd*
early	*neetuhl*
eat	*roda*
evil/bad	*ehda*
face	*jeejee*
far	*eleeoth*
far away	*bok chuu-ock*
father	*deej*
fire	*siz*
flower	*luufi*
food	*manna manna*
foot	*jadgreh*
forest	*eekeekeek*
forward	*ando*
free	*che*
friend	*jeerota*

from	*kla*
give	*ehshtee*
glider	*hveetin*
good	*thees*
ground	*x'eef*
guard/watch/protect	*x'ekra*
hands	*greh*
happy	*drik*
hear	*akeeata*
heart	*teeket*
help	*chyasee*
here	*thek*
hit	*ruha*
house/home	*weewa*
how	*kash*
hurt	*seefo*
I	*meechoo*
important	*x'iutha*
in	*zeeg*
journey	*treekthin*
jump	*yayath*
kill	*e s'eesht*
knife	*tuhkuh*
listen	*arandee*
long	*eetee*
look	*yeek*
magic	*azar*
map	*reshee*
maybe	*danthee*
medicine	*fektur*
monster	*graks*
moon	*chiutatal*

more	*etke*
mother	*shodu*
mountain	*churee*
name	*sheeu*
never	*eleeo*
now	*sta*
nut	*yungyet*
old	*yeh*
on	*seeg*
only	*teera*
open	*yehk*
out	*zehg*
over	*eedada*
parents	*shodeesh*
peace	*yehan*
pit/hole	*tyor*
pixie	*luka yit*
plant	*feef*
pond	*heth*
pull	*aahrgutcha*
push	*geetch*
quick	*veek*
quiet	*t'hesh*
rain	*ooba*
ready	*kra*
rejoice	*yupyup*
rock	*thuk*
route/path	*chees*
run	*treekveek*
sad	*glek*
safe	*zeekee*
safety	*zeekeethin*

say/tell	*yekyit*
see	*yuhyi*
send	*stusl*
shelter	*gooka*
show	*enya*
sick	*drin*
sing	*lulalar*
sister	*freet*
sit	*shtehk*
sky	*uuta*
small	*yigit*
soon	*sut*
soup	*chek*
spaceship	*eedada huutaveet*
spear	*klektuhkuh*
stars	*luka*
stay/remain	*danileeay*
stop	*ileeay*
stranger	*tyehtgeethin*
sun	*tal*
sweet	*oodeef*
take	*eeyaya*
teach	*hurga*
that	*jeeks*
them	*chaa*
there	*thesi*
thing	*yit*
think	*lang*
this	*jiks*
throw	*thleek*
tree	*thu ka kee*
tribe	*na-chin*

truth	*theesdarat*
try	*eechik*
under	*eedeedee*
up	*uhree*
vine/rope	*shtek*
wait	*fudana*
warrior	*shetai*
water	*ah-ah*
we	*ees*
what	*kush*
when	*keesh*
where	*enenah*
who	*kush*
why	*esa*
wind	*ikirath*
you	*weechu*

5 | COMMUNICATING WITH WOOKIEES

Wookiees originate from the planet Kashyyyk, and their language is technically classified as Shyriiwook, though in everyday speech we often refer to Shyriiwook as Wookiee-speak. Wookiees communicate with a special set of sounds, which are subdivided into the following categories:

- Grunts
- Barks
- Waa-waas
- Moans
- Whimpers
- Trills
- Snarls
- Growls

Since the Wookiees were treated as Imperial slaves for many years, and their liberation as a culture has only been recent, Shyriiwook is not a familiar sound to many life-forms in the galaxy. And because of the growling and guttural nature of their speech, Wookiees are generally misunderstood. Except for a few errant groups of smugglers and insurance marketeers, Wookiees as a whole are friendly and sensitive beings, with a rich history and cultural heritage worth learning about. Take my advice—it will do you good to get to know a Wookiee. Learn some basic Shyriiwook.

GETTING STARTED

Many travelers have attempted the most difficult
task of imitating these sounds, but realistically, making yourself understood in Shyriiwook can be very
frustrating and particularly irritating to your throat,
let alone an impatient Wookiee. Usually no more
than six "syllables" per phrase make up a Wookiee
sentence. Many Wookiees comprehend Basic and
Huttese, so resorting to your knowledge of these
languages might get your information across.
However, here are some basics to get you started
when meeting a Wookiee.

To speak in Shyriiwook, open your mouth, lock it
open, and try not to use your tongue at all in forming sound. No lips either. All sound emanates from
the back of the throat. Let's start with a casual conversation.

Hello. How are you?
Wyaaaaa. Ruh ruh.

I am well, thank you.
Wyogg, ur oh.

I am a friend.
Ruh gwyaaaag.

Can I buy you a drink?
Huwaa muaa mumwa?

Nice weather, eh?
Wooo hwa hwa?

Pardon me, I need to rest my neck muscles.
Whoaaaa. Waa maa. Warrgh.

Good-bye.
Yuow.

Just another note: Wookiees also understand many basic gestures in Galactic Sign Language (GSL). A polite greeting is to place your open hand palm down under your chin. Point your fingers and wiggle them at the Wookiee. Make a slight bow of the head.

Wookiees are just plain impatient creatures. If you find you are not getting through to one, and all you are hearing is a rising crescendo of growls, just discreetly *back off.* Give the Wookiee space to swing his arms around, and wait until things settle. Remember, it's pretty difficult to outrun a Wookiee. If he gives chase, just huddle into a ball on the ground. Wookiees are basically peaceful, so he's not going to throw you onto the nearest rooftop unless you continue to be an annoyance. Let him sniff around your huddled form until he leaves, or you can make peaceful verbal contact, such as:

Peace!
Muaarga!

I think my arm has been pulled out of the socket.
Wua ga ma uma ahuma ooma.

Why did you pick on someone one-fourth your size?
Waa hu aa ma ma a oo gah?

COUNTING IN SHYRIIWOOK

1	*ah*
2	*ah-ah*
3	*a-oo-ah*
4	*wyoorg*
5	*ah wyoorg*
6	*hu wyoorg*
7	*muwaa yourg*
8	*ah muwaa yourg*
9	*a-oo-mu*
10	*a-oo-mu wyaarg*

WOOKIEE TRANSLATORS

Recent technical advances in portable and affordable vocabulator assistance have produced the Salespeak 7 droid, which succeeded in translating Shyriiwook into Basic automatically. This has been a great aid to Wookiee comprehension, since their subtle speech phraseology and extensive vocabulary are not appreciated by those that understand only Basic. Although the Salespeak 7 was initially aimed at streamlining the diplomatic process for Wookiees and allowing their representation on the various intersystem councils, there have been a few aberrant commercial uses of the droid.

Most notably, there have been complaints—particularly on Coruscant—of an aggressive holo-marketing campaign that operates over the public comlink system. A translator voice, assumed to be a derivative of the Salespeak 7, autocalls a customer and offers a subscription to the *Coruscant Journal*, with no payments until the end of the season.

Investigation has revealed that this annoyance was launched by an isolated cult of highly aggressive Wookiee marketeers, exploiting the use of the Salespeak 7 on a gullible population, particularly the elderly. This occurred on the very heels of the door-to-door Wookiee suction-droid sales scandal. So it would be wise to learn some basic Shyriiwook so that you can properly deal with the callers.

I cannot talk on the comlink right now.
Mu hu mwa gaa.

It is mealtime.
Uoo waa gaa moo.

I do not want the *Coruscant Journal.*
***Wuyagah na* Kourasaa Yurinal.**

How much is it?
Aa-ooh-gaa?

Please leave me alone.
Mu waa waa.

I already have a suction droid.
Mu ah waa gaa a yukshin oid.

I do not want an in-home demonstration.
My agah ya mawah.

Please go away.
Mu na ya.

SMALL TALK WITH WOOKIEES
Assuming you are in a chair high enough to reach the table, suppose you are having dinner with either

Wookiee business associates or even a typical Wookiee family. Here are some handy phrases to keep you in the conversation:

The food is good.
Waag mam ga moo.

I would like a drink, please.
Wu yaga gah ahyag.

I can't reach that.
Waag ahyeg ha.

Thank you.
Ur uh.

It's hard to find good help these days.
Uwana goya uhama.

How are things at the office?
Hoyaarg aga huwaga?

Think it is going to rain tomorrow?
Gu waagaa ahawag?

How tall is that Wookiee?
Uwaga waa mu Woohiee?

Who was that Wookiee I saw you with last night?
Wugaga hu uwamma Woohiee wa-ah?

Have you heard the latest Figrin D'an?
Wuhu wa gaaa ma ma Igra Ann?

How do you give your fur that shine?
Yaag ruggwah maw huah huah?

Do you have a salve to kill these parasites?
Yu guwah mah oowhama?

Was he injured?
Guhaw maw ohyah?

When will he recover?
Huaah maw wuwu agah?

GLOSSARY OF COMMON WOOKIEE WORDS

doorway	*haaag*
go	*awa*
headache	*yo agaaha*
how	*yaag*
no	*muawa*
okay	*ohh haa*
what	*wuahh*
when	*huaahh*
who	*muaahh*
why	*ah wu aaa*
yes	*uma*

Hopefully, in the coming years, communication with Wookiees everywhere will improve. The Baobab Work Placement Bureau has been positioning many Wookiees in the corporate sector, has begun offering evening classes in Basic and Shyriiwook, and has launched a campaign demanding that employers provide adequate door height, seating facilities, and cruiser-size beds for these tall, furry specimens.

6 | THE BASICS WHEN IT COMES TO DROIDS

Now we come to one of the most challenging areas for human communication: droids. Fortunately, most droids manufactured either by the Empire or the New Republic are programmed to understand Basic. However, the majority of droids do not synthesize Basic, so communication is only one-way.

The ideal situation for the traveler is to own a Cybot Galactica protocol droid, which can handle the bulk of interdroid communication for you. Rentals of protocol droids are becoming more common, and there are various rental companies servicing the most frequently traveled locations. Only the "midsize" droids are offered, though, and colors are limited.

ORIGINS OF DROIDSPEAK

There are a multitude of electronic code-based droid languages. The earliest talking droids had only a binary language consisting of two sounds, one for *yes* and another for *no*. It was called CBell-1.

Somewhere back about 200 standard years, a breakthrough in programming, made by the cyber-philologist Yperio Baobab, allowed a huge expansion of informational speech content to occur. With installation of the Yperio program, droids could recall and pass on all sorts of sensory-gathered data to other droids and machinery. This type of droid-speak was called Bab-Prime. After a time, a cybersociologist working for the Baobab Merchant Fleet injected into the programming a coded "essence of personality," attempting to give a more interactive human flavor to Bab-Prime. What he created, however, acted as a backbone-entangled computer virus, which ran rampant through the droid population.

Droids interpreted the new code in all sorts of random ways. They took on limited but often uncontrollable personalities. They expressed for the first time a range of "emotions," such as arrogance, irritability, and even a form of kindness and comradeship. Some droid users actually preferred these spontaneous aspects of personality, for they allowed a more satisfying interactive relationship to develop between droid and master. The majority of owners, though, periodically wiped their droids' memory cells to reduce or eliminate entirely this essence of personality. However, no one dared tamper with the overall programming. Consequently, droidspeak flourished and further developed during this period from Bab-Prime into Bab-Neo, or "Babno" as it became known.

COMMUNICATING WITH A DROID

At best, direct communication with most droids is one-way, wherein an organic being speaks Basic to a droid. However, there may be instances in your travels when you encounter a droid that doesn't understand Basic. In that event, there are limited sounds you can produce that will get a droid's attention and communicate some very basic information.

The components of droidspeak are:

- Chirps
- Whistles
- Buzzes
- Beeps

To begin, determine with which class of droids you are communicating. Most travelers learn the visual details that distinguish droid class. Often a hallmark with a serial code is located on the bottom of the feet, treads, or suction plates. Carry a reference guide for hallmark numbers with you. If the droid falls within the 0500–0999 class, you may be able to communicate with it. For security purposes, model numbers outside of this range will ignore Basic or any sounds or sign language you might make. Although such a droid may understand Basic, it has been programmed to respond only to the voice signature of its master, who may want to avoid outside interference that would affect the droid's function or behavior.

If the droid falls within the range of communicables, here is how you may communicate: Start by giving it a friendly whistle, with the intonation following the pitch envelope of "Hey there!" or "Hey, you!"

Once you get its attention, just deal with the facts. Get to the point quickly. Keep it scientific.

Can you help me?
A four-note beep with a step down from the first note, then the last two notes each higher in pitch than the first.

Turn on the power.
Make a single, one-second rising-note beep. Beeeep!

Turn off the power.
Make a single, one-second falling-note beep.

Where is your master?
Make a six-note chirp, falling in pitch in the middle of the notes and forming an interrogative envelope at the end of the statement.

Stop!
Give a two-note chirp and hold up your hand, palm open.

Lower the voltage. You are damaging my molecules!
Make a series of short buzzes with your tongue.
(Your buzzing should be at a pitch distinguishable from those of electrocution.)

Some voyagers about the galaxy carry a reed whistle with them to aid in the mimicry of droid-speak. The popular model is the Baobab Larynx-7. With a little practice, droidspeak whistles, chirps, and buzzes can be generated with such a device. There have been hazards, though. Not long ago some bored, unattended Howler Tree children got hold of a Larynx-7 aboard one of the transgalactic starliners. With it they commanded the entire droid service crew to engage in a cabinwide food fight, forcing the pilot to terminate the flight in the Gulf of Tatooine so that the staff could clean the cockpit windshield. So be cautioned, never let a Baobab Larynx-7 fall into the hands of children. It is not a toy, and should be operated only by adults.

ADDITIONAL HANDY DROID SOUND-PHRASES

Can you repair this?
Four equal-pitch buzzes.

Open the door.
Make a two-note beep and tap on the door.

Close the door.
Make a single beep and tap on the door.

Please help me.
Make a series of high-pitch "whoops."

Emergency!
Make a long, sirenlike wail.

Get help!
Create a staccato series of short rising whistles.

Leave me alone, I will do it myself.
Make a sound resembling the noise "ank" and shoo the droid away.

A SPECIAL NOTE ON DROIDSPEAK ENCRYPTION

I bring this topic up now because many travelers have expressed concern that during the recent and ongoing Rebellion, droids have been used as spies and employed to carry secret data. Involvement with unknown, or stranger, droids has proven to be hazardous. You should be suspicious if you detect a soft raspy tone superimposed acoustically on the normal droidspeak. Often this is evidence of an encrypted message. A droid contaminated in this way should be avoided, or immediately serviced to eliminate the encryption.

It should be noted that droids can have their memory banks erased by a qualified technician at any time. The memory loss can be permanent or time-based, allowing for complete recall at a speci- fied later date. Recent investigations into the alleged encryption of hidden messages in the audio enve- lope of droid speech have confirmed that such a process is feasible and may have been used by elite programmers for secret message transmission and espionage activity. Who these elite programmers are remains a subject of speculation. Some say it is the Jedi who are responsible, but the Baobab Research Council cannot confirm this. We mention it only as a caution to the traveler who may be communicat- ing, renting, or interacting with stranger droids. Astromech R2 units seem the most likely candidates for encryption, and involvement with these models may place you at the heart of some unwanted—and potentially dangerous—intrigues.

There is the other issue involving rumors of the alleged Cult of the Power Droids. Some GNK power droids are capable of speaking in a rudimentary word-based language called Gonkian. Odd reports have come to us describing pairs of GNK power droids going door-to-door in isolated parts of the system and soliciting, apparently, for funding for the cult. If this happens to you, my suggestion is to address them with the following phrase: **Gonk. Gonk. Gonk ko kyenga see.**

This comment should satisfy them and they will leave. A translation of this phrase into Basic is a violation of the Baobab Security Directive 51-C. I hesitate in this guidebook to go any deeper into this issue at this time. I am aware of the immense spiritual meaning and controversy surrounding this topic. Perhaps I can address it more successfully in a future publication.

7 | JAWAS CAN BE YOUR FRIENDS

To most humans, dealing with the Jawas of Tatooine, even the friendlier ones, is a sensory ordeal. The plain truth is that Jawas, no matter how freshly washed, smell like a rancid load of eopie cuds. This odor seems to be inherent to their skin chemistry. Everyone at the Baobab Archives is trained to be excessively tolerant of the diversity of alien habits and associated physical characteristics, and we strive to be unbiased toward any species in any way. However, short of jamming the nose shut with Imperial poxy or donning airtight, self-contained breathing apparatus, those offensive Jawa odor molecules find a way into the sensory system of any breathing creature, sentient or not. Only with staunch discipline can a human maintain full mental focus while inhaling near a Jawa. My only advice is to try to just stare the Jawa in the eyes and ignore the smell. Practice these phrases before each encounter:

Greetings!
M'um m'aloo!

I am a friend.
K'masa nu eyeta.

HISTORY OF THE JAWA LANGUAGE

The Jawa language seems to derive from a common ancestor to the Jawas and the Sand People, or Tusken Raiders, another native life-form on ancient Tatooine. Baobab anthropologists have uncovered skulls of these ancient ancestors, which we have named the Kumumgah. There seems to have been a split in the once singular tribe, resulting in taller and shorter individuals, which led to insult, nomadic separation, and division of labor. The shorter specimens focused on stealing and ferreting, and the taller group on stealing and gambling. Out of this came the modern Jawa as a compulsive scavenger, and the modern Tusken Raider as a brigand and compulsive gambler—their betting and target shooting at the Podraces near Mos Espa are legendary.

The ancient Kumumgah language developed into two very different dialects with radically different sound textures. While the Tusken Raiders' sound is guttural and "coughlike," the Jawa speech retains phonemes and words that humans can learn to speak. However, the language is spoken very fast, and every effort should be made to accelerate your tongue when speaking Jawaese. Vocal tongue accelerators can be used. We recommend the fully natural, organic versions, which have fewer side effects. Taken in pill form, these VTAs will relax the tongue and attached muscle systems.

VTAs aside, before speaking with a Jawa, it would be wise to practice the following phrases over and over, accelerating with each repetition.

Want to buy a used droid?
Utoo nye usabia atoonyoba?

Show me the credits.
Shumeneez un toyneepa.

This is mine, all mine!
A beton nya mombay m'bwa!

Repeat these phrases until you can fire them off twice in less than five seconds. That will give you a taste of Jawa speech and a good workout for the mouth.

MEETING JAWAS

For most travelers, especially those alone in the desert wilderness, the first sound you are likely to hear in a Jawa encounter is "**Utinni!**" which is a battle cry of sorts, a triumphal call to all other Jawas nearby that prey has been located. The cry also is used as a great exclamation, proclaiming great wonder or excitement by whatever impresses them.

Following the battle cry is a call to arms, "**Song peetch alay!**" This is the rallying cry to the Jawa band to converge on the hapless victim or salvage prize.

Most of your dealings with the Jawas will probably involve a squabble over your personal property. Make sure all items you possess are tagged ahead of time and tied on or tied down. If you have a vehicle, be prepared to haggle over its sale price whether you want to sell it or not. It's not a wise idea to point a weapon at a Jawa. Often they will have you covered with a large stun gun. If you do provoke them and get a fully charged stun, they will feel free to scramble off with whatever gear you have. Once you regain consciousness, a good stunning will leave you thirsty and your vision will lack all color. Be patient, these effects will wear off after about ten standard hours.

But you should do all you can to avoid a stun, and that involves learning some basic phrases:

Greetings.
M'um m'aloo.

Yes.
Ibana.

No.
Nyeta.

Stop.
Sabioto.

That is mine.
Mombay m'bwa.

MOMBAY M'BWA

Hands off!
Togo togu!

Don't shoot!
Ny shootogawa!

Give it back!
Tandi kwa!

Let's go. Go!
Ashuna! Ashuna!

I want to trade.
Etee uwanna waa.

How much for this?
Go mob un loo?

How much?
Mob un loo?

Too much.
M'gasha.

I won't sell.
Ya e'um pukay.

This is not for sale.
Yanna kuzu peekay.

Let's make a deal.
Yukusu kenza keena.

Okay.
Mambay.

Good day. Good-bye.
Ubanya.

JAWA NUMBERS AND MEASUREMENTS
Most likely you will get into some sort of trade and
bartering with the Jawas, since their drive to swap
and ferret runs so high. Therefore, some knowledge
of their numbering system will be essential.

Interestingly enough, Jawas measure distance by
the size of their clan. Before the advent of sand-
crawlers, when an entire clan was on the move, the

Jawas marched in single file. The length from first to last Jawa in the line became the kuba, their basic unit of measurement, and the custom took hold. Therefore, a value of one hundred kubas is equivalent to one hundred times the length of a clan's tribe lined up. This value can vary widely depending upon which tribe or clan you encounter, so unless you have other sources of information available, be cautious when estimating any distance in the wilderness based on Jawa-supplied data.

COUNTING IN JAWAESE

1	*po*
2	*ko*
3	*kyo*
4	*yo*
5	*dyo*
6	*lyo*
7	*Does not exist in Jawa arithmetic!*
8	*ho*
9	*toe*
10	*kisewa*
100	*gakisewa*
1,000	*hakisewa*
100,000,000	*jo jo muma*

RENTING FROM THE JAWAS

There have been reports of numerous competing rental operations run by enterprising bands of Jawas located on the Salt Steppes of the Dune Sea on Tatooine. It seems they have fixed up a fleet of banged-up repulsorlift craft for use as short-term rentals. The vehicles

are wired and welded together in the most haphazard
fashion, but are functional and relatively reliable.
These vehicles have been a great convenience for
mineral hunters, explorers, campers, and other visitors to that desolate but mysterious region.

Reports indicate the Jawas are relatively fair in
their dealings, but have a warped propensity for hidden charges that often forces the renter into unexpected debt upon return of the machine. The day my
brother-in-law rented, for example, he saw two previous customers working off their bills by curing bantha
hides with their teeth in the adjacent junkyard shop.

Any traveler renting from Jawas should arrive
armed with key phrases:

I would like to rent a speeder.
Ikeena mee koosa ha speeda.

Does it have air-conditioning?
Ushabia namba kee koolee?

Is this an A6 or full A8 repulsor in-line power plant?
Ikeen nwab ba Ah-lyo ooh Ah-ho peetwooza?

I will be returning in ⸺ days.
Ikee weeza tuputa ⸺ baba.

I will take the insurance.
Ikee go cona.

I will not take the insurance.
Ikee nyeta go cona.

How far to ⸺?
Kuminee bok cuza ⸺?

Do you offer road service?
Kuh kiminay po luza?

Where is the nearest fuel station?
Ookwass dok pundwa keenah?

Does that include unlimited mileage?
Ogama ho miketa keezo?

GLOSSARY OF COMMON JAWA WORDS

above	*tiiba*
always	*gomjam*
bantha	*ugama*
bargain	*bom'loo*
below	*nufuzu*
broken	*ko lopo*
burn	*ha'mfoo*
cave	*kiizci*
chant	*hazamuzee*
city	*jubinloo*
clan	*ayafa*
clean	*meeglay*
cliff	*dikwass*
cloak	*lampuka*
cloud	*kiluyak*
cold	*oko*
cook	*bazzok*
credit	*toineepa*
deal	*kenza*
desert	*waff'mla*
down	*doobe*
droid	*usabia*

dune	*rillo*
Dune Sea	*Lika Rillo*
empire	*umpee*
encampment	*cirkoza*
enemy	*hunya*
eopie	*peope*
equal	*ysas*
far	*bok*
fire	*m'wechuk*
fix	*tando*
food	*sooga*
friend	*eyeta*
give	*opawi*
go	*ashuna*
help	*kasita*
here	*junlopak*
high	*ogo*
hole	*m'nuta*
hot	*wass*
how	*buja*
I	*ikee*
junk	*dooka*
knife	*ratapa*
large	*jar k'osa*
later	*yaytah*
less	*loma*
long	*oto*
long ago	*kebee'oto*
low	*kavi*
machine	*ikee kone*
market	*upezzo*
mine	*m'bwa*

mirage	*k'sama*
money	*pop'nloo*
more	*gad'wa*
mountain	*bopom kova*
music	*yazz*
near	*kupu*
never	*nyeto*
now	*kwat*
oasis	*homeo*
okay	*mambay*
patina	*shee neko*
planet	*lum timinee*
pray	*perupa*
price	*umbazz*
profit	*mibbu*
repair	*kurruzza*
restraining bolt	*peeta*
run	*gogowa*
rust	*rubac*
sail barge	*lo'wassa*
sand	*ton ton*
sandcrawler	*kreebaza*
scanner	*dook'wab*
shoes	*fabuza*
short	*wee-jawa*
sing	*oomlay*
sky	*heega*
sleep	*shanay*
small	*meek jawa*
smell	*parufah*
smoke	*vopuba*
spare parts	*opakwa*
speeder	*speeda*

stars	*lopima*
steal	*m'tuske*
stop	*w'ho add*
storm	*opazum*
sun	*wamoomaz*
swap meet	*mee toga tagu*
take	*m'yawa*
thanks	*taa baa*
them	*chikua*
there	*jol*
today	*kiik*
tomorrow	*takiik*
tool	*m'yatak*
torch	*jumlaa*
trade	*uwanna waa*
trash	*da biota*
Tusken Raider	*Tooska Kobana*
up	*okka*
vaporator	*vapoosza*
village	*krallaza*
walk	*umka*
warm	*pibboz*
water	*n'lappu*
we	*ekee*
weapon	*keeza*
what	*m'kwat*
when	*m'tima*
where	*ookwass*
who	*koo*
why	*m'gwaa*
yesterday	*eetiik*
yours	*neng ooka*

8 | SAND PEOPLE OR WORSE

The chances are you will never meet Sand People (Tusken Raiders) socially, or be introduced politely at a cocktail party. Most likely your encounter will begin with the crack and ricochet of a warning shot across your path. Don't dive for cover. They will take this as an aggressive move, and unless you are prepared to trade a fusillade of fire, lower your weapon. Throw your hands into the air. Listen for the wheezing barks and cries from the dunes or rocks nearby to echo away. They will come to you.

You can try the standard **yaa-yaah** peace greeting when they appear. They are not murderers, but raw, uncouth animals. They prefer to intimidate and rob. The peace greeting might soothe their anger, and reports indicate that if you can calm them down, they will often leave your shoes—but little else. Still, shoes are better than nothing, especially on rocky Tatooine, and rather than worry about the likely sunburn on previously unexposed sections of your outer tissues, you should be thankful, humble, and go about resuming your trip.

Should you try to converse in Tusken, lower the pitch of your voice as much as possible. Try to growl and grunt as you form the sounds from the phonetics that follow. You make these sounds by conjuring up

91

a wheezy bark. It is best to practice this at home before entering Tusken territory. A lot of phlegm will help.

Greetings.
Aargh.

I come in peace.
Ru rah ru rah.

I surrender.
Hu raka.

Please leave my clothes.
Eyak ur urah gu.

That time calculator belonged to my mother.
Arg yowr rakak quaraka.

In the rare instance that you get the upper hand on a Tusken Raider, can disarm him, or catch him off guard, here are some useful phrases:

Don't move!
Urrak!

Hands up!
Orukak!

Drop your weapon.
Oru uru kak.

I mean you no harm.
Eyaak urk urk.

Where is the nearest water?
Urrr urah urah urah?

Which way is the nearest settlement?
Iurak ip ip hurak?

To end an awkward encounter like this, the rec-
ommended procedure is to take away the Tusken
Raider's footwear, thus stranding him to some
extent and giving you time to get a sizable head
start if he chooses to pursue. Removing the power
pack from his weapon also gives you a bit of an
advantage, but stealing it is not a good policy, and
should be considered only if you feel truly threat-
ened.

Tusken Raiders often have some rudimentary
understanding of Huttese and Jawaese, since their
habitat brings them into frequent contact with
these groups. Therefore, you can resort to those languages as a possible alternative.

9 | UNDERWATER WITH THE GUNGANS

Gunganese is one of several languages mostly understandable to someone fluent in Basic. For example:

Greetings, I come in peace.
Mesa greeting. In peace mesa comen.

I would like to visit your city. Can you guide me to it?
Mesa liken to visit yousa city. Can wesa goin there?

However, there are frequent convolutions in grammar, and the interjection of some purely Old Gungan vocabulary can make comprehension difficult. Therefore some study of this language is necessary before the traveler can expect truly effective communication.

OLD GUNGAN

Old Gungan goes back a thousand years and originated in the deepest and most remote underwater cities on Naboo. However, based on the fact that Gungan feet are cloven, Baobab historians believe that the ancestors of the Gungans originated on the swampy prairies surrounding the Naboo lakes. Massive herds must have galloped across the plains, and ancient accounts describe the great Gungan migrations as visible from space. The ancient Gung

Slabs, inscribed with Old Gungan on one side and
Old Corellian on the other, have given the Baobab
anthropologists the key to translating Old Gungan
and better comprehending the Gungan speech of
today. A wise suggestion for any visitor would be to
memorize a stanza of Gungan poetry from these
ancient writings. As a bonus, it will make a favor-
able impression at the dinner table with a typical
Gungan family. The following, from the epic poem
Ode to the Central Core, is titled "**O Depu Epu Sea**"
("Deep Dark Water"). It would be hard to match the
incomparable pathos revealed in this ancient epistle.

Oomesa pa Guna mer muda.
  J'ai bongo do deepu sea.
  Mesa hearta go tippy-tap.
  J'ai bongo do deepu sea.
  All dha Gunga wail an gnash,
  No bomba, no crashen . . .
  J'ai bongo do deepu sea
  . . . Tank yu.

At some point an ancient ancestor to the modern
Gungan must have plunged—or carelessly tripped
and fell—into a lake and begun an amphibian existence. The lakes are filled with tasty underwater
grasses, and it must have been this feature that kept
the Gungans immersed until they made a complete
transition to underwater living.
  Baobab anthropologist Burro Flats was first to
visit and put into writing a limited dictionary of
Gungan terms. He also was first to bring back the

Gungan secret of the osmotic membrane, the self-
sealing "bubble" that houses the Gungan underwater structures. He made a fortune when he reversed
the process, creating the patented Rolling Moisture
Cell, which greatly economized the transport of
water by the desert trade caravans of Tatooine.

VISITING THE GUNGANS

The Gungans have a history of scholarly excellence,
which has remained unknown to outsiders to a
great degree because of the difficulty of reaching
their submerged habitat. However, free dives to
these opulent Gungan cityscapes are becoming more
common once again, since the end of the Rebellion.

The Gungans are proud and hospitable beings
who offer an unusual opportunity for the visitor to
be enlightened by a fresh and unadulterated culture.
They take great pride in their underwater world and
refer to it as **"Da Beauty Al'Round."** By our standards, however, they are clumsy, so don't overreact
if dishes are knocked off the table, or unexpected
pratfalls accompany even the most solemn rituals.

Several items are essential for the traveler on a
Gungan visit. First, an underwater breath mask will
allow for respiration during the liquid segment of
your journey, and second, a portable hyperbaric
chamber or bag will be necessary for decompression
when rising from the underwater depths. A too-
rapid ascent from a Gungan city can twist your flesh
into a rather painful gundarkian knot.

Another critical item to consider bringing along

is a standard taste inhibitor, to be digested in tablet form. Take one before each meal. Gungan food is extremely bitter and sulfurous, due to the chemosynthesis rather than photosynthesis that produces their vegetable foodstuff. Infused with volcanic sulfur, Gungan food can be downright putrid and repulsive, especially their favorite, gumfish. A supply of taste inhibitors will deaden your taste receptors and allow you to smile and appreciate the meal, rather than suffer the indignity of clutching your throat and grimacing until your facial muscles are numb.

Although more expensive, taste converters are now becoming more popular than the inhibitors. This medicine will offset the taste receptors in your mouth toward flavors more to your liking. These tablets have actually become somewhat of a craze, with the most popular being the "Ribs of Bantha" converter. Reports from our lab show that even a meal of greased scurrier thorax can be given mouth-watering attraction with the appropriate PTO (Popular Taste Offset).

Some of the most important Gungan phrases relate to meals—for example:

Thank you for the invitation to this meal.
Tanken yousa per da meal invitateon.

Pass the liquid, please.
Oh passa pleasa da liquid.

This is good food.
Dis foosa isa berry good.

May I have more, please?
Mesa wanten more, pleasa?

Thank you. I am full.
Tanka yousa. Mesa am berry fool.

If something is spilled on you:

That's okay, I will get it cleaned.
Dast okeyday. Mesa get it da cleansa.

COUNTING IN GUNGANESE

1	*una*	6	*seeks*
2	*duey*	7	*sevin*
3	*dee*	8	*ate-a*
4	*foosa*	9	*ninee*
5	*fife*	10	*tenska*

COMMON EVERYDAY EXPRESSIONS

As noted, many common Gungan expressions will sound familiar to most travelers.

Most speakers of Basic, with a little practice, can comprehend most of what is said to them in Gunganese, save for the occasional purely Old Gungan word. Here are some of the most common phrases you may encounter:

Hello.
Heyo-dalee.

Hi, there!
Hidoe!

Oh boy!
Oie boie!

Oh, my, my.
Oyi, mooie, mooie.

Okay.
Okeyday.

I don't know.
My no know.

Yes.
Yesa.

No.
No or *nosa.*

Excuse me.
Ex squeezee me.

I'm not doing anything.
Mesa doen nutten!

What did you say?
What yousa say?

I am your humble servant.
Mesa yous humbule servaunt.

I love you.
Mesa luv yous.

Thank you.
Tank yu.

GLOSSARY OF COMMON GUNGANESE WORDS

beeg buba	watertight dome in Gungan architecture
bodooka	energy ball
bo-ganya	dome-shaped force field
bongo	a Gungan underwater transport craft
boopjak	a big mistake
doopeewee	landspeeder or other repulsorlift land craft
ecouch-eee	Gungan chair or bench
farseein	electrobinoculars
feetwalken	floors in Gungan architecture
ganya	sky
garbareeno	garbage or waste
gasser	a Gungan stove
Grandee-Oola	Gungan Council Chamber of Judgment
hata hata	exclamation meaning "Oh my goodness!"
heyblibber	a luxury bongo

huffmaker	wind
keeclumbsee	good manners
logreena	forest
lopity-pie	kaadu fodder
Nocombackie Law	a law that prevents a banished individual from ever returning to a Gungan city
Oma-Oma	principal Gungan deity
ome-goosa	deep ocean depths
opadda	fire
paddlewompy	swimming underwater
sheesh	rain
skeebeetle	spacecraft
spark-ouchee	force pole with an electric shock coil on the tip
stickgooshy	swamp
toboo nuki	affectionate term referring to spouse or children
tongue-grabben	eating
umi-yumi	Gungan dessert made with sulfured fatfish

wangzapper	laser gun
whizbooma	Gungan energy ball catapult
yanzawa	Gungan cavalry charge

10 | EXPOSING YOURSELF TO THE NEIMOIDIANS

Thanks to its ancient association with the trade routes and merchant activity throughout the galaxy, the Neimoidian tongue has spread almost everywhere, and you cannot travel far without encountering it. Its roots can be traced back even further than Old Corellian, though modern Neimoidian has become inextricably mixed with Basic. Still, many older words and expressions hang on.

The pure Neimoidian tongue is tough to master and often difficult to understand. The reason for this is both anatomical and historical. The mouth and lips of a Neimoidian have a very restricted range of movement when compared to most species. Privately, most Neimoidians, especially those remaining isolated on their home planet, will defer to their original form of nonverbal communication, called **Pak Pak**. This form of speech is produced by modulating a steady-state stream of "croaks," and the speaker will do so by varying the shape of his or her throat cavity. When two or more Neimoidians are engaged in **Pak Pak**, one hears a chorus of staccato guttural croaks of infinite and subtle variety. There is a certain musical beauty to it, especially when hormones are running high.

Historically, as the Neimoidians ranged out from their home planet and developed the extensive commerce network that now dominates the central system, they found that **Pak Pak** just couldn't be reproduced or understood by other races. They came to the realization that, in order to hold sway over the myriad of business franchises and trade contracts they controlled, they would have to adapt. Therefore, they forced their rigid vocal cords to mimic Basic, which resulted in the dialect that is most commonly heard today. Some Neimoidians still have trouble understanding Basic, though, and unless you adhere to pronunciation that they consider normal, communication may prove difficult.

There are a number of key spoken Neimoidian phrases that will prove valuable in such instances:

Greetings.
L'a heeting.

Welcome.
Wahr koom.

Good-bye.
Kood b'vy.

I am your humble servant, sir.
Myo yu h'umble zh' ervant, l'ard.

Thank you. (very rare, considered archaic)
Ranka yu.

I will consult my legal adviser.
M'yo vovam consulta cohort.

Payment is required upon delivery.
Pay eez pon del riva.

Tax, of course, will be added.
Taz, uv cosa, be addad.

I have brought the contract.
Myo 'ave brawd da contrak.

I need more time to consider the deal.
E'ee neet moor tyme cho consider da deel.

While the Neimoidians struggled with speaking
Basic, a consistent enough dialect developed that
most offworld Neimoidians have come to use.
Living with a Neimoidian for a spell is the best way
to accustom yourself to the accent and rhythm of
this speech, and having a Neimoidian exchange student in your home for a season may be one of the
best ways to acquaint yourself with the language.
However, there are major risks to housing a Neimoidian. For example, the height of the ceilings in your
dwelling may pose a problem. Even a midlevel student will be at least two meters tall, and so it will be
helpful to master phrases such as:

Mind your head!
Mind yo hyead!

Do you need a bandage?
Do va needa eh bandaga?

The ceiling lamp can be replaced.
Dyo ciela lamp con be repaced.

How's the weather up there?
Howda reather up zere?

The best way to perfect your accent is to practice keeping your countenance rigid, and to move your jaw and lips as little as possible. Occasionally, words of purely Neimoidian origin will find their way into the conversation. The origins are often obscure, and many began as mispronunciations of ancient Huttese and Old Corellian terms. Here are several common words and phrases you should know:

trade agreement
dleefnarc

torture chamber
shanatram

trade show
dleef yrag

bribe
d'nooby

donation
fo d'nooby

force field
forz fowa

contract
contrak

Fire! (weapons)
Kagwe!

fool
dwarfnut

laser blaster
bwasta

lawyer
cohorta

trade embargo
trod umbarga

spacecraft
spabcrak

Drop your weapon.
Drof yo rehpon.

Don't shoot!
Donc chooze!

I surrender.
E'ee zuranda.

COUNTING IN NEIMOIDIAN

1	**von**
2	**thoo**
3	**vree**
4	**voor**
5	**vyiiv**
6	**six**

7	*zevan*
8	*ate'a*
9	*nine*
10	*taen*
20	*teventee*
50	*vivtee*
100	*wunhunard*

Recently an intriguing new Neimoidian handheld vocabulator has appeared on the market and is doing brisk sales. The device simulates the steady chorus of croaks that are the backbone of purely native Neimoidian speech. When you place the active viaphram of the vocabulator into your mouth, you can "shape" your speech into the modular croaking sounds of Neimoidian speech. More and more space travelers are trying this, with great success.

Full details of its use and a *Sound Guide to Native Neimoidian* come with purchase of the vocabulator, and the Baobab Archives offers evening classes for training with the device. I have many pleasant memories of taking a twilight stroll and being transfixed by the tranquilizing serenade of a full class of trainees, their rhythmic chirps and coughs wafting up the stairwells and echoing through the lonely corridors of the Archives.

Some comments should be made relating to the possibility of open hostility with a Neimoidian. The tenuous peace that prevails over much of the galaxy can, as we all know, erupt into violence and strife without warning, and the dominance of the Neimoidians in the Trade Federation has frequently placed them in conflict with various species and sovereignties. The Neimoidians can be ruthless and aggressive. On a one-to-one basis a Neimoidian is not very strong—hence their reliance on droids— and can be overpowered by a fit human. Most Neimoidians rely on cunning and economic forces to suppress their enemies. You may have to rely on more than physical strength to overcome their aggressions. Again, key phrases may provide an advantage:

Hands up!
Aands zup!

Where is the escape pod?
Ver iz da ezkapa pud?

Deactivate your droids.
Deaktivot yo droidhas.

Jettison the cargo.
Jetizzon da kargoz.

I have your ship in my sights.
E'ee ave yo ship in myo zights.

Surrender!
Zuwenda!

Retreat!
Retweet!

DEAKTIVOT YO DROIDHAS.

Of course, it should be mentioned here that the Neimoidians are notorious virus carriers. Although immune to most harmful microbes themselves, they have been the scourge of the galaxy, responsible—although they deny it—for the Great Pandemic of Deersheba and the equally lethal Intestinal Revenge of Bars Barka that created the massive weight loss that swept through the Ubese colonists. For years it has been sarcastically proclaimed that the principal export of the Neimoidian home planet is Brainworm Rot Type C. So many cases have been reported that, at the time of writing of this guide, the Neimoidian home planet has been officially quarantined and is off limits to travelers.

Should you run afoul of a Neimoidian virus, remember the key phrases:

I do not feel well.
Myo not fee werr.

Is there a doctor nearby?
Ees a doktur ear?

I would like to lie down.
Myo vould rike to rie down.

I need to go to the waste collection chamber.
E'ee nee to go to da vatstu datsa.

Baobab historians have concluded that many of the Neimoidian claims to power have been the result of deliberate infection, which weakened any ambassadors or negotiators who were so unfortunate as to enter Neimoidian chambers. So be advised: Wear a breath mask, an enviro-suit, and gloves, and get your immune system fortified.

GETTING A HAIRCUT

Assuming you have hair, this short chapter has been included to aid you in efficiently and effectively getting a shave, haircut, or hairdo. As you may know, the renowned Barbers of Sullust have acquired all the major central system franchises, displacing the Wookiees as the dominant force in the sartorial arts. This is odd, for as everyone knows the Sullustans are a hairless race, and who should know more about hair than Wookiees? Regardless, it is quite important to know some simple Sullustan phrases, in order to achieve the desired removal or rearrangement of the hair on your outer surfaces.

How much for a hair trim and removal?
Kippe h'moo kay ta m'ha?

Take a little off the top, please.
Utu rupee to tupee.

Take a little off the bottom, please.
Utu rupee to bootee.

I'd like my body shaved and shined.
M'ho towhunee moonee end zigwa.

Just clear the breathing holes, please.
L'ko I'ya oot me hoot.

I'd like it raised off the ears.
M'ho tuni voogoo.

I'd like it raised above the antennae.
M'ho tuni jo-jobap.

Just raise it above the holster.
M'ho holta pah noil'ya don.

May I have it curled?
K'a m'ho kurlee hurlee?

I'd like to have it streaked and tipped.
M'ho tooka jooked un rooked.

Give me the standard Wookiee cut.
Jima ja mooska wa Wookiee moo.

Blocked, not tapered.
Mokk, na bazdu.

Tapered, not blocked.
Bazdu, na mokk.

Trim the bangs.
C'hoo za pokeluka.

I'd like my head shaved.
A'foos mak bubon h'iok.

I'd like my head shined.
A'foos mak bubon zigwa.

Shave, please.
O'x na att.

Don't cut it too short.
K'ying goh k'wang see.

Cover the gray.
Naqua zo grinko.

Cover the green.
Naqua zo hapnuk.

I need my roots done.
A foo ma gooptaka bok.

PART TWO

BEHIND THE SOUNDS

by Ben Burtt

For twenty-five years I have lived and worked in a world of imaginary sound. The task of sound design for an episode of *Star Wars* usually involves at least a thousand recording projects. Each noise, from Luke Skywalker's boot in the mud of Dagobah to the fiery explosion of the Death Star, requires a specific act of audio conception. Some sounds, like footsteps, are created by recording something closely related to the reality of the noise. But that monstrous exploding battle station may require a lion roar or a diesel horn as an essential component.

In the end, all final sound effects are added after filming and editing is completed. The sound designer creates an artificial world, and has complete control to select and orchestrate just the right blend of noises for a desired emotional effect.

I look back over notebooks filled with my ideas and notes, and I read entries such as "Weird cry, take horse whinny at half speed and mix it with itself in reverse." I don't know where this flash of an idea came from, but it ended up being the basis for the frightening cries of the mynocks, flying reptiles who attacked the outer hull of the *Millennium Falcon* in *The Empire Strikes Back*. I also spot a large note to remind me to record "seaweed ambience." I can't remember if I ever did that, but it sounds fascinating nonetheless.

My collection of sound has sustained a career of constant adventure: I've drained swimming pools to get the moans of stranded walruses, had tracer bullets pass five feet from my forehead, and hung a microphone over my snoring wife's lovely but unconscious form in search of yet another alien vocalization. I've gone from the Amazon to Alaska to add to my sound files. I've spent months—and a few times, years—in the pursuit of the ultimate effect.

Some sounds, like the lightsaber—fashioned from an old movie projector motor hum and a TV picture tube buzz—came immediately to mind when I first read the script for *Star Wars* and saw the concept artwork. Other challenges, such as the voice of R2-D2, I struggled with for months before I finally hit on something that began to have credibility and character. After all, R2-D2 had to play in scenes alone with Alec Guinness!

Overall, the creation of alien languages has been the hardest task. A language, or more accurately, the *sensation* of language, has to satisfy the audience's most critical faculties. We are all experts at identifying the nuances of intonation. Whether we understand a given language or not, we certainly process the sound fully and attribute meaning—perhaps inaccurate—to the emotional and informational content of the speech. Our minds are trained to recognize and process dialogue. The task, therefore, of creating a language is all the more difficult because of the strength of the audience's perception.

My first assignment from George Lucas back in
1975 was to come up with a voice for Chewbacca. I
was handed an early draft of the script. I turned the
pages and was overwhelmed by the soundscape laid
before me: I not only had a Wookiee, but I had
beeping droids, Jawas, Tusken Raiders, cantina creatures, Greedo, banthas, and, of course, R2-D2. "Do
you want me to collect sound for all of this, too?" I
inquired. "Yes, we need sound for everything. Just
go ahead" was the command.

Well, here I am a quarter century later, still "just
going ahead" with whatever new frontiers in sound
each episode may bring. Behind me is the massive
lexicon of now familiar *Star Wars* images and sound.

But how did it all begin?

Speaking in Tongues

With regard to languages, the sound design began
with research and recording. I divided the work into
three general categories: languages that were composed of animal sounds, those that were derived
from human-produced sound, and those that were
synthesized from acoustical and electronic sounds.
Armed with my Nagra III tape recorder and a microphone, I began collecting in earnest.

Chewbacca's speech is a prime example of a language created by editing and blending animal
sounds. It was George Lucas's idea to investigate
bears as a possibility for the basis of Wookiee
speech, and so I proceeded to locate and record
examples of bears. I listened to stock recordings in

various sound effects libraries, but the noises were of poor quality and too limited in range for development into "speech." I set out to record captive bears. Immediately I encountered the basic difficulty in recording actual animal sounds—they never vocalize on cue. How many times have I gone to a zoo and stood by the pen of a bear or a lion for hours and gotten no sound except the flies buzzing around an inert, sleeping mound of fur tucked into a niche in the animal's enclosure. Nothing could make these sedate, captive animals talk.

My luck began to turn, however, when I began to search among the menageries of trained Hollywood animals. I visited an animal farm run by trainer Monty Cox near Tehachapi, California. He owned a young cinnamon bear named Pooh. With the help of his partner, Susan Backlinie—the bold stunt actress, by the way, who was eaten in the opening scene in *Jaws*—I spent a day inside a pen with Pooh "talking." Being a youthful animal, Pooh loved to eat bread soaked in milk, and Monty had delayed his feeding until I arrived. When food was finally presented for the bear to see, but withheld for a moment, Pooh began to cry, moan, and bleat for it, giving me a good range of sounds to work with.

Accompanying me as boom operator was my friend and former University of Southern California schoolmate Richard Anderson. At one point, the friendly bear stood up on his hind legs, wrapped his arms affectionately around Richard, and completely immobilized him. It was a true bear hug, and I will never forget the look of frozen terror on Richard's face. But Pooh turned out to be a real teddy bear, and he played and rolled around in the dust like a pet dog most of the day.

Another way of getting Pooh to vocalize was to parade other animals past his cage. Monty would walk by with a mountain lion on a leash, and Pooh would "comment" on the intruder, sometimes cowering in fear.

The true value of the day's recordings wasn't truly measurable until I got back into the editing room. I extracted each of Pooh's vocalizations and copied them into categories that, to me, had a common emotional connotation. Some bits sounded happy, or angry, or inquisitive. I was able to build up a word list. I could vary the speed and pitch of these sounds mechanically while copying from one tape recorder to another. I could run sounds in reverse, and edit together little pieces of sound. I found I could create an intonation envelope by stringing different "shape" sounds together, thus giving an emotional meaning to what was otherwise somewhat random. By splicing and pasting together copies of these phonemes—the sounds that are the building blocks of speech—I could create the sensation of short sentences and vocal reactions. If Chewbacca needed a comment that sounded angry, I would pull from my angry list. If Chewie needed to ask a question, I would pull from my collection of interrogatives. I didn't approach the creation of words in a literal fashion, trying to analyze and synthesize diphthongs and triphthongs. Instead, as has always proved appropriate with alien dialogue, I created just the necessary impression of real speech.

As wonderful as they were, I found that the bear sounds weren't quite enough to get the full range of expression I needed for Chewbacca. I recorded several other captive bears to add to the collection, as well as many other mammal noises. At Marineland in Long Beach, California, I happened to be on hand when they drained the walrus pool for routine cleaning, stranding the animals temporarily on dry tiles at the bottom of the pool. This was great for me because all the previous attempts at recording walruses had been compromised by all the sloshing and splashing sounds of their water habitat.

The two beached specimens groaned, whistled, and barked, and I was able to add those sounds to my Wookiee word list. I also recorded various dogs, lions, and seals to augment the bear recordings. Friends caught word of what I was doing, and I would make house calls to collect one performing pet after another. Usually the bulk of the recording would consist of the friend begging the animal to make a sound, and a lot of paw scratching on linoleum with slurpy breathing. Once in a while I would get an isolated unusual bark or moan. One insanely aggressive dachshund was later turned into the massive rancor beast in *Return of the Jedi*.

The development of the sound for Chewbacca also had to take into account the animation of the mask worn by the performer Peter Mayhew. He was restricted to just a one-dimensional opening and closing of the mouth. He couldn't shape the lips, nor did the mask technology at the time include wires or motors to warp the facial surfaces to add expressiveness. Whatever sound I imposed on the face had to be anatomically credible with what movement the viewer saw. Fortunately the animal sounds were consistent with the limits of Mayhew's animation. The bear sounds, in particular, were formed in the back of the mouth, without lips or tongue modulating the speech, and thus conformed nicely to the type of speech the mask was capable of mimicking.

I cut together samples of the Wookiee speech prior to the actual shooting of the movie. Acceptance of these sounds gave everybody confidence that the concept might work, and the sounds provided a guideline for George Lucas and Peter Mayhew to follow. When the actual filming took place, Peter moved the mouth as best he could. He also occasionally spoke his lines in English under the mask to provide the other actors cues for their reactions. This only added to the bizarre nature of the raw soundtrack of *Star Wars* in its earliest incarnations. We seem to take it for granted now, but back then there were some genuine fears that this whole idea of talking aliens and creatures would never work. The very first dialogue in *A New Hope* is between two talking droids, without mouths. One is beeping, and they're in the middle of a battle. This was a very bold way to set the stage. However, after the success of the droids and Chewbacca in the first film, and with the acceptance of the concept of animal speech, even Peter Mayhew began to imitate the growls and barks he heard in the dub. He incorporated them into subsequent performances, and became a full-fledged Wookiee.

Of course, his acting and body language were so unique, you could hardly separate Peter from Chewie. I sat with him in a motel Jacuzzi after hours one day during the shooting of *Jedi*. Somehow he had folded his Wookiee limbs into this little hot

Ben Burtt recording Pooh the Bear for use as Wookiee-Speak.

tub. When a child who had dropped a toy into the pool wanted someone to submerge and retrieve it, Peter just reached down and plucked it up without even getting his chin wet. Wow, were his arms long! It was a moment in which I wished I could have a Wookiee sidekick. It would be so useful, and Peter's natural congeniality brought out the best in a lovable Chewbacca.

Wookiee speech continued to evolve throughout the production of the original trilogy and various other *Star Wars* venues in records, television, and radio. The biggest surge in development came with the production of the rarely seen *Star Wars Holiday Special* in 1978. This TV event required the creation of a whole family of talking Wookiees, including Chewbacca's spouse, Malla, son Lumpy, and grandpa Itchy. I was faced with creating and sustaining a whole hour of Wookiee conversation. I went out collecting again, this time to the Olympic Game Farm in Sequim, Washington. They had a dozen or more captive bears of various species, and I spent two days getting them to vocalize. Actually, one of the best sounds I got while recording there was that of a lion eating a cow's head. That sound found itself in some sound design I did for *Alien*, but that's another story.

Grizzlies provide a basis for grumpy old grandpa, some black bears for Malla. For Lumpy I needed something cute, and I eventually found what I needed at the San Jose Baby Zoo, where I recorded a baby bear named Tarik. At one point I went back to record Pooh, the original Wookiee, but Pooh was now an adult, rather dangerous, and he just snarled at me. Gone was that cute, plaintive toddler who had been the inspiration for Chewie's voice.

Going Backwards

The second major challenge in *Star Wars* language development was to use human-produced sound and the mimicry of actual languages. The goal was to come up with something entertaining, alien, and full of appropriate character.

The very first time I tackled such a problem, I was twelve years old, and was making a drama on audiotape. I wanted to create talking Martians, and I accidentally discovered that if I twisted the tape in my recorder and recorded through the base on the opposite side, then corrected the tape and played it back, I could reverse a sound. If I talked, I could play back the dialogue—backwards.

Backwards talking was okay for Martians, but the idea wasn't new and had been used, in fact, for the Rock People in the serial *Flash Gordon Conquers the Universe*. But I wanted to take it a step further. I postulated that if I could mimic the backwards dialogue that I heard, record my attempt to speak backwards, then reverse that recording, I might end up with something strange enough for Martians. I found this to be more difficult than I imagined. I recorded the phrase "I am from the planet Mars," reversed it, and then practiced saying it as I heard it in reverse. Of course, backwards speech has some impossible-to-imitate characteristics. You find yourself slurping and sucking vowels and consonants and behaving as if you were choking on a peach pit. The results are definitely weird, with intonation all distorted and many words sounding like you are a tongue-deprived Roman galley slave.

Anyway, I found it so hard and time-consuming that after spending hours on one line I gave up. I tried the idea again while working on the

Neimoidians in *The Phantom Menace,* but it just didn't
fit, was once again very difficult, and didn't pay off.
I've found language development to be fraught with
more dead ends and failures than any other category
in sound design. Someday I'm going to make this
backwards-backwards idea work.

Voices from Space

Returning to the early development of alien speech
in *Star Wars*, I listened to recordings of many foreign languages and found inspiration among many
that were entertaining and exotic to my ears. I auditioned language sample tapes from university linguistics departments. I combed through recorded
language lessons and even monitored shortwave
transmissions from around the world just to get
ideas. I especially enjoyed listening to shortwave,
because the aberrations and distortions of speech
produced by sidebanding and mistuned transmissions gave me many ideas for electronic processing.
These I exploited along the way.

As a child I used to spend hours listening to my
grandfather's ham radio receiver. He had built it in
the early 1930s, and it looked like a prop from Dr.
Frankenstein's laboratory. It was set up in his attic,
and when I would visit his home in Ohio during sti-
flingly hot July vacations, I would lose myself under
a pair of headphones, slowly turning the big glow-
ing tuning dial and listening in awe to the electronic
shimmers, beeps, whistles, and modulated voices
that streamed in over the airwaves. The attic reeked

of ozone and hot insulation from the racks of tubes and transformers that magically brought this chorus of alien sound to my ears. I made a few precious recordings just for fun way back then, which I treasure and have used and reused for many *Star Wars* sound effects.

Part of my research was to identify interesting real languages to use as a basis for alien ones. The advantage of using a real language is that it possesses built-in credibility. A real language has all the style, consistency, and unique character that only centuries of cultural evolution can bring. I found that if I relied on my familiarity with English, my imagined "alien" language would just be a reworking of the all-too-familiar phonemes of everyday general American speech. I had to break those boundaries, to search for language sounds that were uncommon and even unpronounceable by most of the general audience.

To this end I searched and found several fascinating possibilities. First came Huttese, which I needed for Greedo when he confronted Han Solo in the Mos Eisley cantina. I heard some recordings of Quechua, an ancient native language of Peru. Some phrases had a comic rhyming. It had a musical intonation. There were smacking sounds and clicks not a part of common speech or of any of the familiar Romance languages. I collected recordings of Quechua and searched for someone who could speak the language.

Out of this research came a linguistics graduate

student from Berkeley. His name was Larry Ward, and he already could speak eleven languages, though Quechua wasn't one of them. But Larry was gifted with the talent of mimicking any language. He could listen to Quechua, and then reproduce a stream of sound that would convince you he was speaking fluently. In fact, it was all double-talk, and this was a major discovery for me.

I got together with Larry and reviewed all I had in Quechua. We wrote down the sounds phonetically, invented and derived new sounds based on what we liked, and did some free-form recording sessions. From this activity, Huttese emerged. Once a collection of favorite words and phrases existed, I sat down and carefully studied Greedo's mouth movements in the cut scene. I wrote out phrases and recorded with Larry specific sentences that were timed to Greedo's movement. Having Greedo speak a humanlike language wasn't actually George Lucas's first choice. At first Greedo was supposed to speak with an electronic, insectlike sound. Then for a while, he spoke in a staccato "oink-oink" language that was created by George and me "oinking" simultaneously into the microphone. The fake Quechua came late in the process.

After recording a good take of each line and editing it to fit Greedo's snout movement, I made two identical loops of each line. I would play the two copies back in sync, then drag my thumb on the reel of one copy, knocking it a few milliseconds out of sync. The blend of the two slightly out-of-sync

recordings produced a phasing effect, or "comb filtering," as it is also called. It gave the sound a tubular
quality that was consistent with a sound generated
in Greedo's long snout. The result was immediately
a hit with George and everybody on the crew. Pretty
soon everyone was greeting each other in the editing room with the phrase "**Koona t'chuta, Solo?**"
At that point I knew we had a success with Huttese,
but I never realized it was going to be taken so
much further in the subsequent films.

Little Aliens, Big Voices

The other big language challenge in *A New Hope* was
the voicing of the Jawas. Their mouths weren't visible under the dark hoods, so lip sync wasn't an
issue. However, body language in such an instance
becomes all the more important. I've discovered
over the years that a voice needs to sync with body
movements as precisely as it does with lip movement, in order for the sound to most effectively
bond with the character. Fortunately, the Jawas were
performed with a lot of animation with which to
link the sound. But what sound?

In all my listening research, I had been drawn to
several African tongues because of the exotic
rhythms and the occurrence of phonemes not
found in general American speech. Zulu was a particular favorite, and I recorded several individuals
who spoke the language. My approach in a recording
survey like this has always been to put the performer—
almost always nonactors—at ease by engaging them

in conversation. In particular it was helpful to have them tell me childhood bedtime stories or familiar folktales where they would dramatize a range of emotions and even play different characters. One individual gave me a really good dramatized argument between husband and wife, which became the basis for a lot of Jawaese. I also remember going down a recording checklist on which I had listed the different emotional states I wanted to record. I would instruct a performer to tell me a very sad story or an angry or excited one. One brave Zulu male balked when I asked him to say the dialogue with fear in his voice. He told me that a warrior such as himself would not know any fear, so certainly he could not express it. I guess that's why the Jawas, despite their size, became so fearless.

Once I had collected a lot of Zulu, I then brought in actors who could listen to the recorded voices and augment the phrases with more specifically articulate performances. I didn't want to just copy Zulu, but to derive from it a pattern and set of vocal sounds based on how *I* heard Zulu. These words and phrases were written down in a little script for performers to read. Most of the recordings were then sped up to raise the pitch and accelerate the flow of words.

To make the voices more authentic, I recorded many of them outside on location so that the echo of the voice would match the acoustics of rocky desert locales in the film. I went with good friend and fellow USC film student Rick Victor to Vasquez

Rocks, a county park in the foothills south of the Mojave Desert and the site of many classic western, adventure, and even science fiction films. In the quiet of evening we set the tape recorder and mike on the ground, and then went up into the rocks and yelled Jawaese phrases like "**Utinni!**" until we were hoarse. The voices had a nice echo and slap off the rocks and, when dubbed into the soundtrack, helped the Jawa vocals seem all the more natural. This location recording was similar to a process suggested by George, which he called "worldizing"— the playback and rerecording of studio voices in real locations to give them a specific reverberation quality that matched the acoustics of the setting in the film. I remember many hours playing back Darth Vader's voice in offices, hallways, and bathrooms, in order to get just the right acoustic quality. These sessions invariably had to be done late at night when no one was around to make noise, the buzz of fluorescent lights could be switched off, and the phones wouldn't ring. It was spooky being all alone, mike in hand, recording Vader's voice booming from the end of a darkened hallway.

Alien "Character Actors"
The remainder of alien voices in *A New Hope* consisted of a potpourri of processed animal sounds with occasional processed human speech mixed in. A hippopotamus provided the "laughter" for a cantina alien. A spring peeper tree frog became another cantina vocal. I had a friend read Latin and chopped

the sound up in a synthesizer to create another weird voice.

One of the more oddball experiments was a recording session of a talking crowd, all of whom were breathing helium. Several crew members volunteered: Lucy Wilson, Bunny Alsup, Michael Kitchens, Howie Hammerman, and Todd Boekelheide. Everyone had a balloon full of the gas and, on cue, inhaled it, then tried to engage in speech. I say *tried* because at first all I would get was the hysterical laughter as everyone reacted to the high-pitched nasal voices. But by take four, they were capable of sustaining conversational tones. I recorded the females only as a group, and then slowed them down in playback to drop the pitch. I recorded the males separately and then sped them up in playback to raise the pitch. By mixing these two components together, I created a "cantina walla," that is, a nonspecific babbling of voices used for a background texture.

People did tend to get oxygen-deprived during the recording session, which added a certain tipsy realism to the cantina babble.

I also filled a closet full of helium, with several dogs inside. My hope was to get a pitch shift upward of whatever sounds the dogs would make. The only result was the sound of angry scratching at the door as the canines demanded their release from the closet. In retrospect, this was a stupid idea, but I was a bold young experimenter back then. Today you can do the same trick digitally without risking any embarrassing respiratory emergency involving your friends, your dog, or your friend's dog.

Probably the most significant use of animalistic sound, other than for Chewbacca, was for the Tusken Raiders. They were labeled as the Sand People in the original film, and that term, although disused now, has always stuck with me. This is due to Luke's famous phrase from the film, "It could be Sand People, or worse!" Paul Hirsch, one of the picture editors, used to chide the sound editors when they arrived for work or a meeting with a twist of that phrase, "It's sound people, or worse!" This affectionate put-down was later embodied in a T-shirt printed just for the sound crew, which depicted a Tusken Raider holding a boom pole and microphone above his head instead of the gaffi stick. We sound people were bonded.

Anyway, the sounds for the Tusken Raiders were inspired by the odd and often chilling donkey braying the crew heard in Tunisia during the location shooting. Donkeys were used to pack the tons of film equipment into the remote locations. Occasionally they would burst into barks and screeches during the shooting and be audible in the background of a take, thus ruining it. But their vocals echoing off the canyon walls proved weird and scary, so they were recorded and sent back to me. I added more to this collection back in the United States and incorporated some other elements of animal breathing and wheezing. Cut and blended together, the result was the speech of the Tusken Raiders.

R2-D2: The Biggest Challenge

For a period of six months, the sound design for languages progressed simultaneously with my development of the sound effects and the progress of the film editing. During that time, one challenge that simply would not resolve itself easily was the invention of droid speech.

There was little or no precedent in cinema history for droid languages. Most robots had spoken English or were mute menaces. Some, like Robby in the classic *Forbidden Planet*, had a normal voice intercut with various mechanical noises and electronic tones, but no filmmaker had tackled the idea of strictly electronic communication.

The real difficulty in bringing R2-D2 to life was creating a sense of character, feeling, and intelligence, using only nonverbal sounds.

I started out experimenting with the various music synthesizers of the era, like a Moog or an ARP. With them I could generate plenty of electronic beeps and tonalities, but the sounds unto themselves were very machinelike. They lacked emotional meaning. This is an underlying issue with all sound effects.

The success of all sound design depends upon the designer's skill in selecting the right sound for the right moment. All sounds bring with them an association with something emotional. Music is the perfect example. No matter what music you play during a scene, it has a significant effect. It might not be what the filmmaker wants, but it exerts its

Burt recording walruses at the bottom of their swimming pool.

power nonetheless. The same phenomenon occurs with sound effects. You search for the sounds that not only bring a sense of naturalness and reality to a film scene but also—and more importantly, one discovers—provide the appropriate emotional association. For example, you can pick out any number of wind backgrounds that will bring a scene very important emotional coloration. You can play a "friendly wind," or a "lonely wind," or a "spooky wind," depending upon the sound texture you have chosen. Sound effects have their own musical qualities, as well.

The same holds true with R2-D2. His nonverbal sounds had to communicate just the right feeling.

R2-D2 had to be warm and alive. R2-D2 had to perform. R2-D2 had to act alone in scenes with Alec Guinness and be credible and believable. This was the challenge.

So I began to add mechanically generated sounds to the electronic. Blowing through a small flexible plumbing tube produced some cute whistling, which I could modify by my own performance as I blew. A variety of expressive squeaks and squawks could be obtained by touching bits of metal—particularly coins—to a chunk of dry ice. The coins, even at room temperature, caused the frozen CO_2 to boil away, and the escaping jet of gas squeezing out from beneath the coin made it vibrate at various pitches. This type of sound was used for lightsaber hits, as well.

Intercutting these more "emotional" acoustic noises with the electronic beeps began to give the R2-D2 voice some identifiable character. But the sound was still only a prototype; it needed something more. I had tried many blends of electronic and mechanical sound, but the mix hadn't yet produced the sensation of an interactive, lovable living thing.

It all came down to one frustrating day after playing George Lucas my latest attempt at R2-D2. George began mimicking with his own voice a kind of baby babble, to illustrate a conversation between C-3PO and R2-D2. I found I was responding in kind with a baby babble of my own to indicate the intonation of a phrase. It dawned on us at that moment that the goofy sounds we were making might actually be what we really wanted. Maybe it was as simple as baby talk.

After all, a baby, without using words, can by vocal noise and intonation communicate an astonishing range of feeling and desires. Why not use baby sounds and mix them with the electronic? I immediately made some sample recordings of babies, but this was harder to do than one would think. You need to hang around a baby and record a lot of tape, on the chance you might get a few usable sounds. Babies don't stay still for the microphone: They thrash about and make unwanted clothing and bedding noises. They don't take instructions or direction of any kind. They want their mothers. They cry when you stick a microphone in their face. They remain silent and smiling for thirty minutes, then babble complete sentences the moment your tape runs out.

I finally realized it was going to be more practical just to make the noises myself. After all, I had once been a baby. I knew what to do.

Closing my editing room door and curling up in a quiet corner with the tape recorder and mike, I began to generate baby talk. I put myself into the mind of an infant and acted out a scene with a droid's intentions in mind. I was periodically interrupted, as always occurred in my sound design room, by noisy footsteps on the kitchen floor above my room. For at this point in time, I was occupying a space in the basement of George Lucas's house, and while I was recording, people would come clomping through the kitchen above without any warning. As a result, many of the sounds in *Star Wars* contain low-level footsteps, the refrigerator door opening and closing, and plates of cheese puffs being carried off.

I made my noises slowly and in a medium-pitched voice. Then I played back the tape at higher speed, making the pitch rise and the speed of delivery accelerate. As silly as it was, as basic as it was, it was immediately successful in capturing and generating a range of performances that were appealing and full of character. I tried intercutting my baby talk with the electronic tones, and that was even more promising, because it blended the machinelike character with the baby babble. However, I found that these two basic elements, the electronic and the organic, needed to be very closely orchestrated and timed so they melded into one voice, rather than sound like two separate sounds.

I devised a means of playing the music synthesizer at the same time as I recorded my voice. In addition, I had my voice automatically trigger electronic sounds and simultaneously shape their envelope. When I vocalized and played the keyboard, I could get a close synchronization with my voice and the electronic tones. If my voice rose in pitch, the electronic would shape itself to conform.

I finally had a working process.

Actually, the first droid voice I generated was for a scene that was eventually cut out of the movie. *A New Hope* in an earlier version included a scene where Luke was in the desert tending to his moisture vaporators. He was assisted by a little droid on tank treads. Luke conversed with the droid, they both watched the space battle in the sky above, and then the droid cried as it burned out and stalled as Luke raced off in his speeder to inform his friends at Anchorhead.

I made up a voice for the little droid and mixed it into the scene. George Lucas loved it, although other crew members thought it sounded more like a talking chicken. In any event, the success of that early sound sketch set the course for the droid voices to come: They would be an interactive blend of synthesized tones and fake baby babble. I embarked on R2-D2 with this new inspiration.

I began with the script. The original screenplay described only in general terms that R2-D2 would beep or whistle. Specific dialogue wasn't written out or developed. When the scenes were shot, there was no noise from R2-D2, except an occasional offscreen voice from an assistant director or script supervisor saying "beep-beep" to cue the other actors. When the scenes were brought back to the editing room and assembled into a first cut, I began developing the real droid voice in earnest.

To aid me in creating logical dialogue for R2-D2, I started out by writing his dialogue in English. His debut dialogue with C-3PO in the Blockade Runner corridor in *A New Hope* would thus read:

C-3PO
Did you hear that? This is madness!

R2-D2
Don't blow your bolts, this battle's not over yet!

Let's head down to A deck for cover.
Darn! They've sealed it off. We can't go this way.

C-3PO
There's no escape for the princess this time.

R2-D2
Don't panic, let's go around and down the back
stairway.

And a little later in the sequence:

C-3PO
At last, where have you been?

R2-D2
Threepio, I've got an assignment, I—

C-3PO
They're heading in this direction!

R2-D2
Okay, okay, but listen.

C-3PO
What are we going to do? We'll be sent to the
spice mines of Kessel.

R2-D2
Enjoy the trip! I've got to get moving. Adios!

Using this mock script as a guide, I developed
electronic sounds for R2-D2 to mimic the emotional
and informational content of these phrases.
I spent many lonely days isolated in the sound-

design basement huddled over a warm Moviola and endlessly chopping and splicing 35mm magnetic film into R2-D2 phrases. I don't think we ever had complete confidence that the voice concept would work, but that was the feeling about the whole project. There were many unknown experiments under way with the whole idea of *Star Wars*. Each of the three picture editors were working on separate scenes. I was taking their cuts and putting in experimental sound effects and voices, and only George was sampling the results of the overall process. No one but me had yet seen or heard any full scene with sound, and no one had yet seen the story put together in sequence. That wouldn't occur until we had our very first screening.

Star Wars: *Screening One*

George Lucas, Gary Kurtz, and the editing crew nervously filled the little screening room. The lights went down, and a beat-up workprint clattered through the projector. I felt like I might be attending an execution.

However, much to everyone's absolute and complete amazement, what flickered before us wasn't the hodgepodge of confusing concepts we feared, but an entertainment storm that broke over us in torrents of fun and enchantment. I got teary-eyed with relief by reel three, forgot I was working on the film by reel six, and was cheering the action by reel seven. We arose after that screening knowing that something far greater than just the sum of each part was brewing. There was still a multitude of sketchy visuals and incomplete sound, but what we saw and heard was astounding. In my heart, I realized this film was good enough that maybe, if we were lucky, we might get invited to the next Star Trek convention in Los Angeles.

History, and the public response, proved otherwise. A phenomenon was created, and I had steady employment for the next fifteen years, bought a home, raised a family, and counted many blessings. I was catapulted into the *Star Wars* universe, with the challenge and pressure to top myself each time a new film was born.

Post–Star Wars

There was almost no new language creation for *The Empire Strikes Back* except for the Huttese insult "E chu ta!" hurled at poor C-3PO by his silver counterpart in a hallway in Bespin. Translating this expletive into Basic wouldn't really be printable in this book. Probably the only other, although relatively minor, vocalization in *Empire* was to be created for the Ugnaughts, the dwarfish little laborers in the junk room and carbon-freezing chamber. Their cries and mutterings derived from a successful recording session with some baby raccoons frolicking in an empty bathtub.

There were a number of new talking droids in *Empire*. The voice of the probot and its mysterious warning transmission came from the shortwave recordings from my grandfather's ham radio, mixed with some outtakes of weird transmission noises I created for *Alien* for the warning signal that beckons the spaceship *Nostromo* to a ghostly planet. Many times, sound trials and errors from one project, which may at some point seem useless, prove to be perfect for a subsequent project. Many of the rejected sounds I made for *Alien* ended up being the basis for all the ghosts swarming out of the ark at the climax of *Raiders of the Lost Ark*.

I've been blessed with so many imaginative soundscapes in the films I've designed for that I think eventually a place has been found in the soundtrack for almost every interesting sound I collected. Sometimes you take excessive pride in making a conscious creative effort through theory and experimentation. Sometimes you just run out of time and you throw the nearest sound on the shelf into the mix. It is those spontaneous choices that often are the most remembered.

When *Return of the Jedi* began preproduction, it was obvious that the biggest new language challenge was going to be Ewokese. It would have to be distinctive from Huttese, which was also going to be significantly present for Jabba and his minions. In addition, there were to be songs in both languages, so there was quite a big job ahead.

I approached Ewokese along a similar tack to that of the Jawas. I first searched for some exotic languages that would act as inspiration. I thought I would start with Tibetan, for I had seen a documentary on public television that gave me a tantalizing sampling. Finding individuals who spoke Tibetan

Burtt in the original sound-design room in the basement of George Lucas's house.

proved to be quite difficult. I located a Tibetan gentleman who ran a gift shop in San Francisco, and he also brought in his father. The recordings were intriguing, but since the men were not actors, it was hard to get performances from them.

As I continued to search about, another unusual individual turned up, an eighty-year-old Mongolian tribeswoman who had just recently, and for the first time, been brought to urban civilization. She spoke no English, but was quite congenial, as long as she

had a desired beverage on hand. We called her
Grandma Vodka, and she spoke Kalmuck. With shot
glass in hand, she exuded some very charming folktales in a raspy high-pitched voice that inspired Ewok.

I discovered that alien voices are particularly credible if the listener cannot clearly identify the age and
gender of the original speaker. This ambiguous quality
relieves the voice from any associative bias. If the
voice is created by a child or an old man, for
instance, no matter what you do, it still will probably be recognized as just what it is. However, I've
found elderly female voices to be a superb starting
point for aliens. I suppose this stems from the success I had in *E.T. The Extra-Terrestrial* using Pat Welsh
as the English-speaking component of E.T.'s voice.
She had a deeper tone than average, and with a little
electronic pitch shifting, her voice could become
completely detached from any age or gender bias.

I tried, in general, the same approach for
Ewokese. From the starting point with Grandma
Vodka, I recorded a number of low-pitched female
voices performing the Ewok vocabulary. A talented
woman with no acting experience named Adeal
Crooms became the voice of Wicket. The words
were a mixture of mock Tibetan, Kalmuck, and even
a bit of Native American Lakota. The principal con-
tributors formed a somewhat poetic roll call: Kosi
Unkov, Lama Kunga, Jr., Lama Kunga the Elder,
M. K. Nepali, Khendup, and Ditry Daza.

When it came to crowds of Ewoks babbling,
singing, and chanting, we brought in a subset of the

Oakland Inspirational Choir. A mixture of talented male and female gospel singers, they readily picked up the Ewok vocabulary and could act in concert under my direction. The ultimate Ewok experience, however, was the performance of the London Symphony Orchestra with the Oakland Inspirational Choir singing the Ewok Freedom Song at the finale of the movie. The song, now retired and replaced in the *Special Edition*, was sung with Ewokese lyrics translated from John Williams's original score. I couldn't help but laugh when I heard what had started with raspy ol' Grandma Vodka coming back to me as the finest vocal sonorities that all Britannia could muster.

Huttese Comes of Age

The biggest character—in more ways than one—to speak an alien language in *Return of the Jedi* was, of course, Jabba the Hutt. George Lucas wrote a few words of Huttese into the script of *Jedi*, including **bo shueda** and **boska**. The rest of Jabba's dialogue in the script was in English and needed translating. This had to be done before filming began so the puppeteers inside Jabba would have a guide for the pattern of mouth movements they were to perform.

I remember, prior to filming, visiting the Jabba's Throne Room set and crawling up inside Jabba. (Guess where you crawled in. It wasn't through the mouth.) I took a turn operating the jaws. My interest was caught by the purr of some musical little servomotors that operated his eyeballs. I made a tape recording of them in action and used that sound years later for battle droid movements in *The Phantom Menace*. Inside Jabba was a smelly, dank place, reeking of glue, latex, and sweat. It actually took, I think, six operators to control his overall movements during a performance.

The voice for Jabba was greatly refined during postproduction, when the scenes were being edited, and dialogue was often rewritten to accommodate new ideas in the details of the storyline. The voice was performed by Larry Ward, who had a deep voice to begin with, but not deep enough. I pitch-shifted his voice as low as it would go and still maintain intelligibility. Then a subharmonic generator was used to derive even deeper tones, almost an earthquake rumble in short bursts, that were mixed in with the words. On top of all this was added a slurpy noise derived from the sound of pasta being fondled in a bowl of my wife's cheese casserole.

For Jabba's big burps, I knew right where to go. For years we had all been held in awe and repulsion by our prime sound engineer's sonorous belches. Howie Hammerman would drink a can of soda and then broadcast the carbon dioxide back to us in bursts of gastronomic thunder. As was the pattern, nearly every interesting noise around us eventually found a place in the soundtrack. We put Howie in front of the microphone, and he gladly added his personal creativity to *Star Wars* sound history. Dialogue editor Laurel Ladevich cut and synchronized all the Jabba elements, including the Howie burps, and mixer Gary Summers dubbed it into the movie.

Another language that was introduced in *Jedi* was Ubese. This was an electronic textured voice for the bounty hunter Boushh, who in reality was Princess Leia in disguise. Once again I called on the voice talents of Pat Welsh. She was a lady living in my neighborhood who I had discovered one day in the local photo store. I was working on *E.T. The Extra-Terrestrial* at the time and was struggling to come up with a concept for the English-speaking component of E.T.'s voice. During a lunch break I went into the photo store to purchase some film. As I stood in line at the counter, my ears were suddenly enlightened by a rather slow and low-pitched voice talking with the clerk about a Visa credit card. The source of this unusual speech was a female senior citizen at the head of the line.

I had learned to take every sound encounter seriously. I cornered Pat on the sidewalk as she exited the store, and approached her with the pickup line, "Pardon me, ma'am, would you like to be an alien?" She didn't balk for a moment. She smiled, looked me in the eye, and delivered the pleasant response, "Sure." We walked the one block to our little editing room and recording studio, I sat her in front of a microphone, and the rest is movie history.

Pat was such a good sport. Her success as E.T. inspired her to speak to groups of schoolchildren and answer all phone calls in E.T.'s tranquil tones. I tried to find different ways to use her deep and airy voice, the product, unfortunately, of chain-smoking since the late 1930s. I auditioned her for Ubese and the voice of Boushh. Once I wrote and recorded the dialogue, I processed her voice with a ring modulator, which created an electronic resynthesis of her words out of an oscillator tone. Ubese was a rather terse language, comprised of short staccato words to distinguish it from all the Huttese spoken in Jabba's palace. Thank the maker for C-3PO, who acted as a continuous translator for all this alien dialogue. Without him I wouldn't have a job, I guess.

Yet another new language in *Jedi* was Sullustan, the language spoken by Lando Calrissian's copilot, Nien Nunb. Pat Welsh led me to a college exchange student she knew named Kipsang Rotich. He was from Kenya and spoke excellent English, as well as his native tongue of Hyah. I recorded him telling folk stories and acting out little minidramas. One thing I did try with him, just for fun, was to actually write out Nien Nunb's lines in English, with their literal meaning as it pertained to the story. Some of these lines were so good in Hyah that they went right into the soundtrack unmodified. This was risky, but I was under tremendous time pressure and I gambled that no one hearing the film would speak Hyah and recognize the language. Was I wrong! And surprised. When the film played in Nairobi a year after release in this country, listeners in the audience were thrilled to hear their own language in *Star Wars*. They took it as a great honor. Kipsang Rotich became a celebrity in his home country and made the rounds of the local talk shows. Fortunately the lines they recognized made sense in the context of the story.

I've had scattered reports over the years of people in very far-off places hearing a phrase that they recognize deep in the soundtrack of *Star Wars*. Tibetans have caught a few familiar words among the Ewoks. Someone in Ecuador, studying Huttese carefully, told me that he heard Greedo say to Han something about the fact that he "loved Han's big blue eyes." Now, that one scared me.

A final comment about *Jedi* should be made with regard to the original Huttese lyrics to the song performed by Jabba's band featuring Sy Snootles. The vocals were sung by a worker in the sound department named Annie Arbogast. She was a most intriguing character. She sang with a local punk band and at the time dressed the part with fireworks-colored hair, spiked wrist bracelets, and vampire makeup. One of her jobs in the department was to run wires from one location in the building to another. One day I came into the mix room, thinking I was alone, when I heard clunking in the floor. I watched and was greatly startled to see the floor panel in front of me crack open and emit a glow of light. I expected the Alien, but no—out popped Annie with a flashlight in her mouth and a long coil of cable in one hand. She was merely arriving from some distant location, having crawled through the bowels of the building with a connecting wire for some new equipment. Anyway, Annie was pressed into service for her singing skills, and she also wrote her own Huttese lyrics in consultation with me. We recorded the song, and until the music was replaced

in the *Special Edition* of *Jedi*, she had been the
Huttese singer Sy Snootles. Last I heard, she had lost
the vampire look and had settled down somewhere
as a soccer mom.

A Twenty-Year Gap

After the completion of the first trilogy, a few *Star
Wars* TV shows, the National Public Radio dramas,
Ewok movies, and *Droids* and *Ewoks* animation
series, sound design for *Star Wars* ended its first
grand phase. Many of us were just plain exhausted
and depleted. At one point I never wanted to hear
another laser blast. I didn't watch the films for a period
of perhaps twelve years. I didn't even encourage my
kids to watch them on home video. I wanted, somehow, for them to see it first, if they did at all, in the
venue for which it was designed—the big screen. It
wasn't until the idea of a twenty-year anniversary
came up, and its subsequent evolution into the
Special Editions, that my excitement was rekindled.

I went to the theater one day and ran all three
films as a little reminder. Frankly, I was a bit overwhelmed. Time and gray hair had given me a new
objectivity. I no longer looked at the films and saw
what had *not* been accomplished: those fallen
expectations compromised by lack of time, technical
limitations, or creative failures. Rather, I saw and
heard all that had been successful. It was inspiring,
and the creative juices began to flow again, along
with an eagerness to tackle the creation of a new
movie, armed with powerful new technical tools.

The New Era

Episode I *The Phantom Menace* was about to become a reality.

As usual, the breakdown of the script indicated that perhaps a thousand recording projects were in order. Actually there were just over 1,300 by the time the film was finished, if you count each new character voice, ambience, piece of hardware, weapon, vehicle, switch click, relay, power generator, pyrotechnic, and droid motor. Once again, Huttese was to be the dominant alien language, and there were a few new but significant voice developments.

My first task was to take lines written in the script in English and translate them into Huttese. I did so, and then I recorded myself performing the lines, as a guide for the actors to pronunciation and intonation. Each actor got a reference tape from which to rehearse.

For the battle droids, the decision from the start was that they would speak English but be electronically processed in some way to make them sound like low-intelligence drones. I had new digital processing techniques at my command, and I developed a set of filtering and ring modulation programs to alter the sound. At one point the idea was to record each battle-droid word separately, out of context with any particular phrase or sentence. Then the words would be joined together as if they were being called up from memory and stuck together by the droid's rudimentary computer. It might have

Ben Burtt, standing, (L–R) Greg Landaker, Steve Maslow, and Bill Varney, mixing **The Empire Strikes Back.**

sounded something like the computer voice synthesis you get over many autoresponding telephone systems.

I did some experiments to create that sensation, but I wasn't happy with the results. The droids lost that elusive dimension of being "living characters." I was reminded of what I had learned with the voice of R2-D2. Machines are not as interesting and involving as something that projects an illusion of will and intelligence. The battle droids needed just a little bit of intelligence, not enough to make them duck a lightsaber swung directly at them, but enough to make you identify with their sense of purpose and will to survive.

So I dropped the single-word synthesis and went back to performed and electronically processed phrases. Although each droid had a different voice, they were all processed to be monotonic in pitch, just to give them a shade of a soulless telephone company synthetic voice.

The language for Jar Jar and the Gungans wasn't really within my realm. Just as he had done with Yoda, George conceived within the script an unusual pattern of speech and vocabulary for Jar Jar. Ahmed Best, who performed the reference Jar Jar on the set and voiced the character, added his unique talents to the performance, filling it out with funny vocal sound effects.

The Neimoidians were a maelstrom of conceptual possibilities. There was a debate at first whether they should be computer-animated beings, or puppet men in masks. The former was possible, but very expensive. The latter was limited, but cheaper. I'm sure it was a tough choice for Lucas and producer Rick McCallum, and they opted to gamble their financial resources on the creation of Jar Jar as a digitally animated character rather than the Neimoidians. They didn't feel they could have both.

For the voices, the problem was bounded on one hand by the limitations and lip sync of the puppet mouths, and on the other by the desired intelligibility of their voices and the critical content of what they had to say. The Neimoidians provided the political and strategic exposition of the storyline. What they had to say was very important. Although it would have been, perhaps, more exotic to give them an alien language and subtitle the scenes, that would have meant a lot of reading for the audience, particularly kids.

I had as one of my digital tools a very powerful sound synthesizer called a Kyma. With it, after a month or so of study and theorizing, I came up with a method by which I could input a normal voice and have it analyzed and then resynthesized using a completely different sound effect as the texture of the voice. For example, I could substitute for the fundamental tones in the normal human voice the sound of water glurping down the drain. Or, I could take a cougar purr and "make it talk." The circuit worked better than I expected, but not well enough. There were just too many little electronic artifacts in the resultant sound to convince George Lucas. He thought it sounded too synthetic. Once again I was reminded of just how critical the human perceptual system is to human speech. In a sense, we are all experts at speech analysis, and this makes the illusion of credible alien voices so very difficult.

Perhaps in the next film I'll get a talking-drain creature.

Versions of Neimoidian speech came and went as we tried different dialects. A funny but never-played-for-George version was one using professional sports announcers for the voices of Neimoidians Nute and Rune. I thought it actually had possibilities. It was so counterpoint to the way they looked. But I was deranged for a while.

Then one day we got a voice-audition tape from Bangkok with trial voices for the eventual dubbing into Thai for release in that market. I really liked the quality of the accent, and we ordered more samples to study. We had a casting call for Thai actors, but mostly what we got were Thai nonactors who just loved *Star Wars*. Eventually we opted for real actors who were adept at dialects and could pattern themselves off the samples of speech we liked. For added flavor, an occasional completely alien word was injected into the dialogue to keep it exotic and characteristically offbeat. I must say that all this was a bit risky, but working in alien worlds always has its hazards.

The bulk of my alien language work turned out to be in the familiar realm of Huttese. Jabba returned, along with the Howie burps. A vast assortment of Podracers and Tatooine alien extras rounded out the requirements. A smattering of pit droids was also required. They were fashioned in the manner of R2-D2, combining baby talk with, in this instance, cute noisemaking toys rather than a musical synthesizer. Despite a whole new palette of digital audio tools at our fingertips, I still find the most successful sounds to be either real acoustic sounds that you encounter in everyday life, or sounds generated in the simplest, most traditional analog means.

As I've said, the key to creativity in sound design is to develop the skill to select just the right sound at just the right moment. Good sound by no means is just loud sound, nor sound in large quantities. It is carefully chosen samples of meaningful noise that relate to some predictable emotional response. Sound doesn't by necessity have to be high fidelity, digital, stereo, or Dolby encoded. All of these qualities are a refinement to the presentation, but nothing beats a simple, well-chosen noise that has emotional meaning. Think of all the classic films that made superb use of a relatively low-fidelity recording and reproduction system. Think of the roars of King Kong, the zinging note of Errol Flynn's arrow in *The Adventures of Robin Hood*. I think of the mileage I got out of an old studio recording of an elephant, which became the TIE fighter. It worked because it commanded an emotional response.

I have fun looking at the walls of tapes that contain years of recordings of *Star Wars* sound effects and voices. On the old tapes the labels are handwritten, and seeing the slightly fading descriptions is very nostalgic. Each tape had its moment in time as it captured sonic modulations that got turned into the fantasy soundscape of *Star Wars*. From *A* for *air conditioner* to *W* for *wind*, there are thousands of noises I've met and become friends with. What a blessing that they all fell in together to form a natural and fully credible alien culture.

Finally, as in most cultures, eventually a need for an encyclopedia and dictionary arise. Hence, this phrase book. Each one of you, by listening to *Star Wars* and picking up a few meaningful alien phrases, becomes a philologist. My hope is that it can be an informative and entertaining document that will make your journey into the fantasy universe of *Star Wars* all the more meaningful and fun.

Goopta mo bossa!*

Ben Burtt
Sound Designer
Star Wars

* Huttese; a traditional farewell idiom literally meaning "May your mind not evaporate."

APPENDIX

SELECTED ALIEN LANGUAGE SCENES FROM STAR WARS

A NEW HOPE
Greedo Confronts Han

Greedo
Koona t'chuta, Solo?
Going somewhere, Solo?

Han Solo
Yes, Greedo, as a matter of fact, I was just going to see
your boss. Tell Jabba that I've got his money.

Greedo
Soong peetch alay.
It's too late.

Mala tram pee chock makacheesa.
You should have paid him when you had the chance.

GALAXY PHRASE BOOK AND TRAVEL GUIDE | 167

Jabba wah ning chee kosthpa murishani tytung ye wanya yoskah.
Jabba's put a price on your head so large every bounty hunter in the galaxy will be looking for you. Ha, ha, ha.

Chas kee nyowyee koo chooskoo.
I'm lucky I found you first.

Han Solo
Yeah, but this time I've got the money.

Greedo
Keh lee chalya chulkah in ting cooing koosooah.
If you give it to me, I might forget I found you.

Han Solo
I don't have it with me. Tell Jabba—

Greedo
Jabba hari tish ding.
Jabba's through with you.

Song kul rul yay pul-yaya ulwan spastika kushunkoo oponowa tweepl.
He has no time for smugglers who drop their ship-ments at the first sign of an Imperial cruiser.

Han Solo
Even I get boarded sometimes. Do you think I had a choice?

Greedo
Klop Jabba poo pah. Goo paknee ata pankpa.
You can tell that to Jabba. He may only take your ship.

Han Solo
Over my dead body.

Greedo
Uth laynuma. Chespo kutata kreesta krenko, nyakoska!
That's the idea. I've been looking forward to this for a long time.

Han Solo
I'll bet you have.

SOLO BARGAINS WITH JABBA

Jabba the Hutt
Solo! Hay lapa no ya, Solo!
Solo! Come out of there, Solo!

Han Solo
Right here, Jabba. Been waiting for you.

Jabba the Hutt
Boonowa tweepi, ha ha.
Have you now.

Han Solo
You didn't think I was going to run, did you?

Jabba the Hutt
Han, mah bukee, keel-ee calleya ku kah.
Han, my boy, you disappoint me.

***Wanta dah moolee-rah? Wonkee chee sa crispo con
Greedo?***
Why haven't you paid me? And why did you fry poor
Greedo?

Han Solo
Look, Jabba, next time you want to talk to me, come
see me yourself. Don't send one of these twerps.

Jabba the Hutt
***Han, Han, make-cheesay. Pa'sa tah ono caulky
malia. Ee youngee d'emperiolo teesaw. Twa spastika
awahl no. Yanee dah poo noo.***
Han, Han, I can't make exceptions. What if everyone
who smuggled for me dropped their cargo at the first
sign of an Imperial starship. It's not good business.

Han Solo
Look, Jabba, even I get boarded sometimes. You think I had a choice?

Jabba the Hutt
Squawk!

Han Solo
But I got a nice easy charter now. I'll pay you back, plus a little extra. I just need a little more time.

Jabba the Hutt
Han, ma bukee. Bargon yanah coto da eetha. See fah luto twentee, ee yaba.
Han, my boy, you're the best. So, for an extra twenty percent.

Han Solo
Fifteen, Jabba. Don't push it.

Jabba the Hutt
See fah luto eetheen, ee yaba ma dukey massa. Eeth wong che coh pa na-geen, nah meeto toe bunky dunko. Lo choda!
Okay, fifteen percent. But if you fail me again, I'll put a price on your head so big you won't be able to go near a civilized system.

Han Solo
Jabba, you're a wonderful human being.

Jabba the Hutt
Boska!

RETURN OF THE JEDI
C-3PO Speaks to the Ewoks

C-3PO
My friends, you must be wondering what all the trouble is about.
Ku channa ma flu-atta. Ku channa ma flu-atta.

Well, we are all escaping from a dreadful person called Darth Vader. *(breathing)*
Coroway manna coo-too, tim nee ah wunday ooss, vu tata rundi Darth Vader.

Fortunately, we did meet another man, named Obi-Wan Kenobi.
Lin chenko vas skeemo. Me-chee un Obi-Wan Kenobi.

May the Force be with you.
May the Force be with you.

And he fought Darth Vader with a laser sword. *(sword sounds)*
Ee manna ma-chu Vader con yum-num.

The swords flashed and burned!
A toy yum nah. A toy yum no.

But suddenly Obi-Wan disappeared.
Obi-Wan me oit tu gaa tay!

And then, they invented the Death Star, a terrible planet.
Oos, a tum da Death Star, hoat taa gu!

I've got a bad feeling about this.
I've got a bad feeling about this.

And Master Luke, very clever, got in his X-wing fighter
(fighter sounds) and flew right up to this Death Star . . .
and then he fired, Bang! and the whole thing exploded.
***N'tse Master Luke a mitchay mitchu. Chimminay
choo doo, Bang! You way day solja.***

It was wonderful. Yes, Artoo, I'm coming to that.
It was wonderful. Yes, Artoo, I'm coming to that.

Then, there was a terrible invention, the walkers, and
they walked in the snow, and attacked us. *(walker
sounds)*
***Coroway manna coo-too . . . toront too gosh,
toront too gosh.***

But Master Luke got in his snowspeeder and he exploded them all. *(snowspeeder and explosion sounds)*
Master Luke tearaway hootu oos-stu-ah-a chimmi-nay choo doo, choo doo. Boom! You way day solja.

Oh my, and then we all got in the *Millennium Falcon* and flew to Cloud City. *(Falcon flyby sound)*
Un tata tull uta* Millennium Falcon *a chimminay Cloud City.

And it was so beautiful there, very serene, but stormtroopers . . . ah my. Don't shoot! Ahh!
Ee tah maruirsa, maruisa, oss, va . . . ahh, oh my, bee choo do can choo do! Ah!

I was shot and everything fell off. My hands, my legs, and my head.
A tull, a aty, ma toto.

But things were worse for Han Solo. He was frozen in carbon, and we thought he was dead. *(carbon-block-hits-floor sound)*
Tall tay bay Han Solo. Tee ka low carbon. Ba moy.

But he wasn't, and we all rescued him and that's how we got to be here.
Aa-oona. Oss, va pa-manna luta.

We've come to seek your aid in fighting these enemies. Please help us.
Baa moit na hay goo-ip too cah. Vade soy oto gubu. Nu wunday, nee a wundy, nee a gro-libu.

Ewok Celebration Music

Freedom . . . we got freedom.
Yub nub . . . eee chop yub nub.

And now that we can be free, c'mon, let's celebrate.
Ah toe meet toe pee chee keene g'noop dock fling-oh-ah.

Power . . . we got power.
Yahwa . . . moe whip yahwa.

Celebrate the freedom.
Coatee-cha tu yub nub.

Celebrate the power.
Coatee-cha tu yahwa.

Celebrate the glory.
Coatee-cha tu glowah.

Celebrate the love.
Allayloo ta nuv.

Glory, we found glory. The power showed us the light.
Glowah, eee chop glowah. Yawah pee chu knee foom.

And now we all live free.
Ah toot dee awe goon-da.

Celebrate the light . . . Freedom.
Coatee-cha tu goo . . . Yub nub.

Celebrate the might . . . Power.
Coatee-cha tu doo . . . Yahwa.

Celebrate the fight . . . Glory.
Coatee-cha tu too . . . Ya-chaa.

DEDICATION

To my Father, Ben Burtt Sr., who had the brilliant
idea of bringing a tape recorder to my bedside.

ACKNOWLEDGMENTS

This book is really the outcome of a movie career in post production sound. I've had the special support both professionally and personally from the following fellow sound artists: Gary Summers, Laurel Ladevich, Howie Hammerman, Andy Aaron, Kris Wiskes, Randy Thom, Bill Varney, Teresa Eckton, Larry Ward, Richard Anderson, Matthew Wood, Buck Rogers, and Flash Gordon. I want to thank you all. I also want to thank Lucy Autrey Wilson, Sue Rostoni, and of course, George Lucas, for your support on this book.

ABOUT THE AUTHOR

Ben Burtt Jr. was born in Syracuse, New York, in 1948. When six years old, a serious illness forced him to stay in bed for several weeks. To counteract his boredom, his father, a chemistry professor at Syracuse University, brought home what was at that time a mysterious new invention: a tape recorder. It was a heavy device the size of a large suitcase. Placed beside his bedside, the machine offered Ben hours of entertainment recording vocalizations and homemade sound effects. Out of this fun came a passionate interest in sound and how sound effects and music was used for dramatic effect in the motion pictures and television shows Ben loved. He became an amateur movie maker at age ten, and made adventure and comedy films with his friends throughout his teenage years. Ben designed a sound track for each film which, due to the technical restraints of the time, had to be presented accompanied by a tape recorder. The taped sound track then had to be manually synchronized at a live event each time the film was shown.

Burtt made several films in his college years that won national festival awards. Although he graduated with a degree in physics, he won a scholarship for a 16mm special effects film he created called *Genesis*. Burtt applied and was accepted as a graduate student at the U.S.C. School of Cinema. As a student, he was incredibly excited by the fact that he now could design a sound track that would stay in sync. Although his interest was in being a director (as were most film students), he developed a special interest in producing sound effects. This work got the attention of *Star Wars* producer Gary Kurtz and when Ben graduated, he went to work on *Star Wars* creating sound effects. For fifteen years he was on staff at Lucasfilm doing sound design and mixing for the *Star Wars* and *Indiana Jones* movies. Becoming independent in 1990, Burtt drifted into a directing career. He directed episodes of *The Young Indiana Jones Chronicles* and several Imax films and documentaries. He won four Oscars for his sound work and six additional nominations, including Best Documentary Short Subject in 1996.

Burtt returned to *Star Wars* as the sound designer and also as a picture editor for *Star Wars: Episode I The Phantom Menace* and the upcoming *Star Wars: Episode II*.

Ben Burtt is married to the fantastic Margaret Burtt, and has four terrific children: Alice, Mary, Benny, and Emma. They sleep, eat, fight, work, love, and grow in character together somewhere near a little creek in Northern California.